He wanted to help her. Even if that meant facing a truth he didn't want to face.

She stood there, her breath hitting against his mouth. Her incredible blue eyes wide with concern.

And with her body pressed against his.

There was a moment, just a split second, when his body started to think below the belt again. A moment where he wondered what it be like to kiss her.

How did she taste?

And were those lips as soft as they looked?

Jackson felt himself moving in closer. His body revved up, everything inside him preparing for something that damn sure shouldn't happen....

DELORES FOSSEN

WILD STALLION

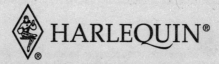

HARLEQUIN®

TORONTO • NEW YORK • LONDON
AMSTERDAM • PARIS • SYDNEY • HAMBURG
STOCKHOLM • ATHENS • TOKYO • MILAN • MADRID
PRAGUE • WARSAW • BUDAPEST • AUCKLAND

Recycling programs
for this product may
not exist in your area.

ISBN-13: 978-0-373-69515-7

WILD STALLION

Copyright © 2010 by Delores Fossen

All rights reserved. Except for use in any review, the reproduction or utilization of this work in whole or in part in any form by any electronic, mechanical or other means, now known or hereafter invented, including xerography, photocopying and recording, or in any information storage or retrieval system, is forbidden without the written permission of the publisher, Harlequin Enterprises Limited, 225 Duncan Mill Road, Don Mills, Ontario, Canada M3B 3K9.

This is a work of fiction. Names, characters, places and incidents are either the product of the author's imagination or are used fictitiously, and any resemblance to actual persons, living or dead, business establishments, events or locales is entirely coincidental.

This edition published by arrangement with Harlequin Books S.A.

For questions and comments about the quality of this book please contact us at Customer_eCare@Harlequin.ca.

® and TM are trademarks of the publisher. Trademarks indicated with ® are registered in the United States Patent and Trademark Office, the Canadian Trade Marks Office and in other countries.

www.eHarlequin.com

Printed in U.S.A.

ABOUT THE AUTHOR

Imagine a family tree that includes Texas cowboys, Choctaw and Cherokee Indians, a Louisiana pirate and a Scottish rebel who battled side by side with William Wallace. With ancestors like that, it's easy to understand why Texas author and former air force captain Delores Fossen feels as if she were genetically predisposed to writing romances. Along the way to fulfilling her DNA destiny, Delores married an air force top gun who just happens to be of Viking descent. With all those romantic bases covered, she doesn't have to look too far for inspiration.

Books by Delores Fossen

CAST OF CHARACTERS

Jackson Malone—This Texas billionaire had no idea that the newborn he'd adopted might have been stolen from his birth mother's arms. Now, to protect the child he loves as his own, he must open his door and possibly even his heart to the woman who could cost him everything.

Bailey Hodges—After someone stole her newborn son during the Texas maternity hostage incident, Bailey has dodged danger to try to find him. She hadn't counted on her search leading her to Jackson's lavish doorstep. Nor had she counted on falling hard for the Texas tycoon.

Caden Malone—The four-month-old baby at the center of a police investigation. Is he Bailey's missing son?

Evan Young—Jackson's workaholic business manager who's having a hard time dealing with his fiancée's recent death and with Jackson's new role as daddy.

Shannon Wright—A nurse who worked at the San Antonio Maternity Hospital during the hostage incident. Shannon could be hiding secrets.

Ryan Cassaine—The attorney who handled Caden's adoption. It's possible that Ryan cut corners, or worse, during the adoption.

Robin Russo—A records clerk at the San Antonio Maternity Hospital. She claims she knows nothing about Bailey's missing baby, but Bailey's not so sure.

Prologue

San Antonio Maternity Hospital

"Shhh," Bailey Hodges heard someone say. "If they find you, they'll kill you."

Bailey tried to open her eyes to see who had just spoken that warning, but her eyes didn't cooperate. Neither did the rest of her. Everything felt thick and sludgy.

"Who are you?" Bailey managed to mumble. But someone quickly clamped a hand over her mouth.

"Don't let them hear you," the person whispered. It was a woman. But why had she said that? "If they find you, they'll kill you."

Bailey heard someone else call out her name. Not a woman this time, and the person sounded angry. Or something.

What was going on?

She was in the San Antonio Maternity Hospital. There shouldn't be anyone shouting for her. She shouldn't be in danger.

Bailey forced herself to think. It wasn't easy. She'd just come from surgery where she'd had a C-section because her baby had been breech. The doctor had tried to give her an epidural, but when it hadn't taken effect, she'd been given a general anesthetic instead. It had knocked her out completely.

"My baby!" Bailey tried to say, but the hand stayed clamped over her mouth.

Bailey struggled as much as she could, but her arms and legs wouldn't cooperate.

"Your son is safe," the woman said.

"Son," Bailey mumbled. She had a boy.

"Stay quiet," the woman warned. "They're close to us now."

Bailey didn't know who "they" were, but the man calling out her name was indeed nearby. He sounded right outside the door. Oh, God. Was he really going to try to kill her? If so, she couldn't fight back. But she had to do something to protect her baby.

"I have to leave," the woman said. "It's the only way I can keep your baby safe. Do you understand?"

"No." Bailey didn't understand. "What's happening?"

"Gunmen have taken the entire ward hostage. If I don't get out now, they'll find the baby. They might hurt him to get to you. Hush, or you'll get us all killed."

Bailey shook her head and managed to force her eyes open. She still couldn't see clearly. Everything was swimming in and out of focus, and she could barely make out the woman, or rather, her outline. But Bailey couldn't see her face.

She heard the sound then. Not the man yelling for her. Not the woman. It was a kitten-like cry, and she instinctively knew it belonged to her baby.

"My son," Bailey mumbled.

The woman slid her hand away from Bailey's mouth

and hurried toward the door. She didn't tell Bailey where she was going, but Bailey could see that the woman had something in her arms.

A baby wrapped in a blue blanket.

The woman ducked into the hall and disappeared.

Bailey tried to scream, to tell her to bring back her son. But she remembered the warning.

"Hush, or you'll get us all killed."

That robbed her of what little breath she had, and she felt the tears burn as they slid down her cheeks. She was helpless. Too weak to move. Too drugged to do anything to stop this nightmare.

Bailey had no choice. Her eyelids drifted down, and the darkness took over.

Chapter One

Four Months Later:
The Malone Estate, Copper Creek, Texas

Jackson Malone watched the woman from the surveillance monitor on his desk. She was either the most inept Christmas tree decorator in the state, or else...

Jackson didn't want to go there yet.

By nature, he wasn't a trusting man, and now that he had become a father his distrust was stronger than ever. That probably had something to do with the threat he'd received just that morning.

He glanced at the letter, the warning spelled out in letters cut from magazines.

"Jackson Malone, I won't forgive and forget. Watch your back."

It was the third one he'd received in the past month. No name. No postmark. The others had been placed on his car windshield, but not this one. This particular letter had been left on the sidewalk outside his downtown San Antonio office building. It'd been a blind spot for security cameras, so there was no footage of the person who had left it for the night watchman to find, but Jackson had some ideas. After Christmas, he'd deal with it.

Or maybe sooner.

His attention went back to the surveillance monitor and the inept tree decorator. The leggy brunette was still trying to untangle some Christmas lights, a task she'd been at for the better part of an hour. She was perched on the lower rung of a ladder next to the ten-foot-tall blue spruce. She had a wad of lights in her hands, but her attention was everywhere but on the task she'd been hired to do. Unlike the others who had accompanied her.

On the split screen, Jackson could see there was a crew on the grounds, decorating the trees and shrubs of his country estate. Another woman was in the great room arranging greenery and crystal angels around the massive stone fireplace. Another pair was on the porch dealing with the door and white marble columns.

So who was this woman on the ladder?

And was she doing surveillance for a robbery, or God knows what else?

He looked through the names of the work crew that his groundskeeper had provided. Her name was either Marita Hernandez or Ann Reeves. Since she wasn't Hispanic, he was betting she was the latter.

Jackson grabbed the phone from his desk and called Evan Young, his business manager. It was three days before Christmas, and Malone Investments was closed for a two-week holiday break, but as Jackson expected, Evan was in his office because he gave new meaning to the word workaholic.

Jackson had once given Evan a run for his money in the hours-at-work department, but since his son, Caden, had come into his life, Jackson had cut way back, not just on the hours, but on his commitment to the job. These days no one could accuse him of being married to his company.

"Evan," Jackson greeted, and even though he was eager to get down to business, he paused and waited for Evan, just in case the man wanted to mention the significance of this particular date.

"No need to call and check up on me," Evan stated. His voice was void of any emotion. "I'm doing fine."

Jackson doubted that was anywhere near the truth. It was the six-month anniversary of Sybil Barnwell's death. She was Evan's fiancée. Evan might be cold-blooded in business, but Jackson knew that the couple had been in love, and even though Evan had refused to take much time off, he'd been devastated by Sybil's death.

And Jackson suspected that, deep down, Evan blamed him for what had happened. Hell, Jackson blamed himself.

"I have a possible problem," Jackson explained. Best to get right onto the business at hand, rather than dive back into those memories of Sybil's death. "Tap into the security feed here at the estate and zoom in on the Christmas tree decorator in the foyer. That's camera eight. Have security run the facial recognition program. I want to know who she really is."

"You think she's connected to the threatening letter left for you this morning?" Evan asked.

"Could be." And that's what he intended to find out.

Jackson ended the call, got up from his desk and headed to the foyer. It was nearly two p.m., which meant

Caden would be up from his nap in a half hour or so. Waking time was Jackson's favorite part of the day, and he wanted this possible situation with the decorator resolved by then.

He went through the maze of corridors and smiled when he thought of Caden again. In another two years or so, his little boy would no doubt be riding a kiddy tricycle around the mansion on these now pristine hardwood floors. He'd be laughing, making noise, and Jackson couldn't wait.

There'd been a dark cloud over this place for too long.

Jackson kept his footsteps light, and paused at the top of the stairs so he could look down at the decorator and observe her in the flesh. She had finally made it to the point where she was actually stringing lights, but her gaze was still firing all around.

She wore jeans and a gray turtleneck sweater. Both nondescript. She definitely wouldn't stand out in those clothes. He could say the same for her short, light-brown hair and her lack of makeup.

"Looking for something?" he asked, his voice echoing through the foyer.

She gasped, obviously startled, and nearly fell off the ladder. Jackson started down the stairs in case he had to pick her up off the floor, but she managed to keep her balance, even though she dropped the lights. Some of the bulbs shattered when they smacked against the glossy marble, and bits of colored glass scattered everywhere.

"I'm, uh, decorating, of course," she said, sparing him a glance. She got off the ladder and onto her hands and knees to gather up the glass bits. "You scared me. I thought you'd be at work."

"I'm working at home today," he volunteered. In fact, he'd been in a business meeting with a client when the decorating crew arrived. It was the reason he was still wearing a suit.

Jackson walked across the foyer toward her, and glanced up at the security camera tucked in the corner behind a sconce. Evan was no doubt watching them, and probably trying to get a good shot of the woman's face so he could process it through the facial recognition program.

"Leave the glass," Jackson instructed, so she would stand. It'd give Evan a better angle of her face. "The housekeeper will take care of it."

But the woman shook her head and stayed down, and she didn't look at him when she spoke. "My boss would fire me if I didn't clean up after myself. Besides, we wouldn't want to have the floor messy when you bring your baby boy in to see the tree for the first time."

Everything inside Jackson went still.

Maybe it was the latest threatening letter, or maybe this was just his paternal instincts yelling out for him to keep Caden safe. Either way, he wanted to know who the hell this woman was.

"Who said I'd be bringing down my son to see the tree?" he challenged.

Her hand froze over a bit of broken glass, and Jackson saw her fingers trembling. That was his cue to reach down, catch onto her arm and haul her to her feet. Her expression froze, caught somewhere between shock and fear.

"I asked you a question," he reminded her.

He put his fingers beneath her chin and lifted it to force eye contact. Finally, here was something that wasn't nondescript. Her eyes were a cool ocean blue. Definitely memorable.

And disturbing.

Jackson didn't exactly step back, but he didn't approve of the way she or her eyes made him feel. There was that hit of attraction, something he didn't intend to feel when it came to her or any other woman he distrusted.

She tried to shrug. "It's in all the newspapers that you're in the final stages of adopting a baby."

"I am." And he left it at that.

"He's four months old, I heard. The right age for really noticing the lights and decorations. Since this is his first Christmas, I just figured you'd bring him down to see the tree as soon as we were done."

That was the plan. But it wouldn't happen with this woman around.

She stepped out of his grip, turned away from him and discarded the bits of glass into a trash bag hung alongside a box of ornaments. "I hope this doesn't sound too personal, but what made you choose adoption?"

Oh, this conversation seemed well beyond personal. "Let's just say I recently had a life-altering experience, and it put things in perspective."

"Yes," she agreed, as if she knew exactly what he meant. "You survived a plane crash about six months ago. I read about that, too."

"You read a lot about me." Though he knew his survival had been a front page story in all the state's newspapers.

He'd been the only survivor among the eight people

who'd been on his private jet when it had to make a crash landing. Evan's own fiancée, Sybil, who was one of Jackson's attorneys, had been killed. So had two of his department CEOs and other employees. They were all on that plane because he had insisted they accompany him to a hostile takeover meeting in Dallas. Jackson, on the other hand, had literally walked away, but he'd walked away a changed man.

A lot of lives had changed that day.

"I need to get something out of the work van," the woman mumbled.

Jackson didn't intend to let her get away that easily. He caught onto her arm again. "Who are you?"

"Ann Reeves," she quickly supplied. Again, she broke his grip.

He stepped in front of her and blocked her path. "Ann Reeves?" he repeated. "Why were you looking around the place as if you planned to steal something?"

Her eyes widened. She shook her head. A thin breath left her mouth. "I would never take anything that wasn't mine. Never."

Jackson expected her to break the eye contact, to try to move away from him again, but she didn't. She held her ground and stared at him. "Can you say the same?" she asked.

Now that was a question he hadn't expected. "Would I take something that wasn't mine?" he clarified. "It depends."

She blinked, her memorable blue eyes narrowing. "You know what I'm talking about."

No. He didn't. Nor was he sure why he'd given her that "it depends" answer. The old Jackson would have said that. And in the past he would have meant it. There'd been a time in his life when he would have acquired property, or whatever he wanted, not through illegal means exactly, but he hadn't been above stooping to down-and-dirty business tactics.

That was before Caden.

Before he'd held his son and had his world and his heart turned upside down.

Jackson was about to ask her to explain her last comment when his phone rang. While still blocking her path, he took the cell from his pocket and answered it.

"Evan," he responded. "What do we have?"

"Well, she's not Ann Reeves," Evan quickly provided. "Her driver's license photo is a match to a woman named Bailey Hodges. She's thirty-four, and her address is on the north side of San Antonio."

Bailey Hodges. The name sounded familiar, but Jackson couldn't put his finger on where he'd heard it before.

"I'll have her background in a few minutes," Evan added, and he hung up.

Jackson put away his phone and got right in her face. "All right, why are you here in my home, Bailey Hodges? Did you leave that threatening letter for me?"

She opened her mouth to say something but seemed to change her mind. "What threatening letter?" And she was too surprised and concerned for that not to be a real question.

He continued to study her. "The one I sent a copy of to the San Antonio Police Department so they could investigate it." That was all Jackson intended to tell her about that matter. "Why are you here?" he repeated.

She didn't answer him. Instead, she took out a folded

piece of paper from her jeans pocket. For a moment, he thought it was another threatening letter, but it was a pair of photographs that looked as if they'd been copied from the computer. She thrust the paper at him.

"Do you know either of these women?" she demanded.

He glanced at the two photographs. They were both strangers. "What does this have to do with you being here at the estate?"

"Everything," she whispered. A moment later, she repeated it.

Tired of this confusing conversation and whatever game she was playing, Jackson stepped out of her way. "It's time for you to leave."

"No."

"No?" It wasn't often anyone said that to him. In fact, he couldn't remember the last time. The woman was gutsy. Or maybe not very bright.

"Look at the pictures again, *please*. Perhaps the hair color isn't the same. They could have done something to alter their appearances when or if you met them. So look hard and tell me if you know one or both of them."

Jackson didn't bother looking at the photos again, and he handed the paper back at her. "I don't know them. Or you. But I do know you're lying about who you are, and I know I want you out of my house now."

She hesitated and then turned as if she might just do as he'd ordered. But she stopped. "What kind of letter did you receive?"

He mentally groaned. "I don't intend to discuss that with you."

More hesitation. "Was the threatening letter a warning about me?"

"What?" This conversation had just taken a more confusing turn. "Why would it be?"

She seemed relieved. Or something. And she waved him off. "I'll go, for now. But I can't stay away. I have to know the truth about him."

Jackson couldn't remember the last time he'd been dumbfounded, but he sure as hell was now. He watched her walk to the double entry doors and wondered if he should stop her and demand an explanation. But his phone rang again.

"Evan," he said, answering the call.

"I found out some things about Bailey Hodges," Evan started. "She's single. A graphic artist who designs promotion brochures and such. She's actually done some work for us. She was engaged, and her ex-fiancé was her business partner, but things must have soured, because he moved to Europe nearly a year ago, and she removed him from her business records."

"She did work for us," Jackson mumbled. "Maybe that's why her name sounds familiar."

"Maybe. But it's probably because she was one of the San Antonio maternity hostages."

Now that did more than just ring bells. Four months ago, a group of pregnant women, new mothers, medical staff and even some babies had been taken hostage by two masked gunmen. They'd been held for hours.

Several people had died that day, including a cop's wife.

That instantly gave Jackson a connection with her. They'd both survived something that others hadn't. It'd been the top news story for weeks, even after the two gunmen and their boss had been captured.

But then Jackson remembered something else about that hostage situation.

One of the newborns had gone missing.

He remembered the Amber Alert that had been issued, mainly because he had been involved with the preliminary adoption process at the time. Even though he'd yet to hold Caden or even know of his existence, Jackson was now fully aware of how heart-crushing it would be to lose a child.

A child that had come into his life just two weeks after the hostage situation and the Amber Alert.

"Yes," Evan said, as if he knew exactly what Jackson was thinking. "Bailey Hodges's baby is the one the cops couldn't find after they rescued the hostages."

Jackson's stomach twisted into a cold, hard knot.

"A coincidence," Jackson mumbled.

"Could be. Caden's four months old. The age is right, but the adoption lawyer you're using is reputable."

Still, it was a private adoption, and there'd been room for some loopholes. None that he knew about.

But that didn't mean there hadn't been some.

That's the reason he'd been checking and double-checking the paperwork. In fact, he'd had a conversation with Ryan Cassaine, the attorney, just the day before. Jackson hadn't wanted to have a problem arise down the road. He wanted to confront any possible issues now, and work them out before the adoption became final in less than a week.

"The lawyer wouldn't have dealt in stolen babies," Evan added. "Ryan Cassaine went to law school with Sybil, and she had nothing but high praise for him."

"Make sure everyone else feels the same about him," Jackson insisted. And he cursed. This couldn't be happening. Caden was his son in every way that mattered.

Bailey Hodges's lost child had nothing to do with them.

Jackson replayed the look in her eyes. The cryptic warnings. The strange conversation. And he prayed he was right—that this was all just some bizarre coincidence that could be explained away.

"There's more," Evan continued. "The cops are concerned about Miss Hodges. She's apparently been conducting her own investigation into her son's disappearance. She's hired someone to hack into files. She's been following the suspects, so much so that one of them got a restraining order."

Jackson shrugged. "Her behavior is understandable. She wants to find her son."

"I agree. But there's more. Not long after the hostage incident ended, someone tried to kill her. The cops think it was the gunmen or their boss."

This wasn't helping his decision to go after her. It was only creating more sympathy for the woman. "But the threat is over, now that the gunmen and their boss are dead, right?"

"Maybe." And Evan paused, the moments crawling by. "The last time she spoke to the cops, she said someone was still following her."

Hell.

"Was the threatening letter a warning about me?" she'd asked.

Now, he understood why she wanted to know. But she'd also told Jackson that she couldn't stay away, that she had to know the truth about him.

Him.

Had she meant Caden?

Cursing even more, Jackson headed for the door so he could try to figure out what was going on. But he got there just in time to see Bailey Hodges driving away in the work van she'd ridden into the estate.

Jackson clicked off the call with Evan so he could phone Steven Perez, his estate manager, and have someone shut the front gates. Bailey Hodges probably wasn't headed to the address on her driver's license, and with her suspicions about someone following her, she likely wouldn't be an easy woman to find. Jackson didn't want to lose her.

But he was damn concerned about who she might really be.

His house manager answered, but Jackson didn't get a chance to issue the order to shut the gate.

"We have a problem, sir," Steven said. "An exterior sensor was tripped, so I checked the security feed. We have an intruder."

That didn't ease the knot in his stomach. "You don't mean the decorator in the van, do you?"

"No, sir. I mean the person who just scaled the west fence on the back side of the property. He's armed, and he's making a beeline for the estate."

Chapter Two

Bailey blinked back the tears. She couldn't cry. She'd save those tears for later. For now, she needed to get off the Malone estate and away from whoever had been alerted because of Jackson Malone's suspicions about her.

Her face had no doubt been caught on a security camera. She'd anticipated cameras of course, but she hadn't anticipated that she would alarm the estate owner to the point where he would have her investigated.

It'd been a huge mistake to come here today.

She wanted to kick herself for not being able to resist the chance to see the baby that Jackson Malone was adopting. Now, her weakness had put her in a position where she had to regroup. Heaven knows how long it would be before she got another opportunity to get back on the grounds and see the baby.

The estate road leading to the highway was a series of deep curves, and she had to ease up on the accelerator. She certainly couldn't risk crashing into one of the massive pecan trees that were on each side of her.

An injury could delay her search.

Bailey spotted the wrought iron gates just ahead. In only a few seconds she'd be on the highway where she could turn onto one of the side roads and get out of sight of anyone that Jackson would send to follow her.

But the gates started to slide shut.

Her heart went to her knees, and despite the danger from the trees, she hit the accelerator. She had to make it through them before they closed. If not, Jackson might have her arrested for trespassing.

Bailey took the last curve, the tires squealing in protest at the excessive speed, and for just a moment she lost sight of the gates. When she came out of the other side of the turn, her heart did more than drop.

The gates closed right in front of her.

Bailey slammed on the brakes. She smelled the rubber burning against the asphalt. Her body lurched forward, the seatbelt digging into her stomach and chest. And then there was the sound. Metal slamming into metal when the front of the van collided with the wrought iron.

The airbag deployed, smacking into her and pinning her against the seat. Bailey didn't take the time to determine if she was hurt. She had to get out of there now. There was a footpath gate next to the wrought iron ones, and she might be able to leave that way.

She fought with the airbag and managed to shove it aside. Maybe because her hands were shaking, getting out of the seatbelt was no easy feat either. She finally got her fingers to cooperate and she disengaged the lock. Ready to run, Bailey threw open the door.

But she didn't get far.

A rail-thin young Hispanic man came bursting through the shrubs and trees. She recognized him. He was with the estate gardening crew who had told them where to put some exterior lights.

He was dressed in work clothes, jeans and a dirt-splattered denim shirt, and with his breath gusting, he caught onto her arm. "Mr. Malone says you're to come with me," he told her. "A man just climbed over the security wall. An intruder."

Oh, God. "Where is he?"

He started to run with her in tow. "He's headed to the main house."

Bailey didn't know how she managed to hold on to her breath after hearing that. Was the intruder after the baby? Was that what Jackson's threatening letter was all about? He was a very wealthy man, and someone might be attempting to kidnap the little boy for ransom.

She had to help keep the baby safe, even if he wasn't hers. And even if it meant putting herself in danger.

Bailey didn't ask where the man was taking her, but she did make sure he wasn't armed. There was no visible weapon, and he wasn't big or strong enough to be hired muscle. If she had to, and she might, she was fairly certain she could fight him off if he turned out to be someone who wasn't concerned about the baby's safety.

They cut through a garden on the east side of the property. The man didn't stop running. Neither did Bailey, though the icy December air was knifing through her lungs and making it hard to breathe. She hadn't put on a coat for her escape, and the chill was slowing her down.

She finally spotted the estate, but the man stopped next to some thick shrubs and checked around them before they ran the last hundred yards across the lawn to an east entrance. It was a sunroom decorated with plenty of lush green plants and pristine white furniture.

"Miss Hodges," someone said the moment they entered.

Jackson Malone was standing there in the opening that divided the sunroom from the main house. Unlike when she'd seen him earlier in the foyer, he'd ditched his perfectly tailored midnight blue business coat and loosened his tie. His storm black hair was rumpled. His eyes were troubled.

And he had a gun pointed at her.

Bailey wanted to scream at herself. How could she have been so stupid? She'd bought the gardener's story about an intruder, and in doing so, she'd come right back to the lion's den.

Jackson looked at the gardener who'd *rescued* her. "Thank you, José. Now go back to your quarters and lock the door. I don't want anyone out on the grounds until we know what we're up against."

The man gave a shaky nod, mumbled something in Spanish and hurried away, leaving Bailey alone with an armed man.

"I would have gone after you myself," Jackson said, as a threat, "but I didn't want to leave my son." He motioned for Bailey to follow him.

She didn't. Bailey stayed put. "Is there really an intruder?"

"There is." His tone left no room for doubt. He held up the sleek, multifunction cell phone he had in his left hand, and on the tiny screen she saw what appeared to be video feed from security cameras. The man was dressed in camouflaged clothing and a ski mask.

And he was carrying an assault rifle.

"My advice?" Jackson added. "Bullets can go through glass, so if I were you I'd move."

She glanced at the sunroom, three sides of which were indeed glass. Still, Bailey didn't budge. Going inside could be just as dangerous as staying put. Jackson didn't have his gun aimed at her exactly, but it was angled so that aiming it would take just a split second.

"Is this some kind of trick?" she asked. "Do you want me dead and out of the way?"

Jackson just stared at her. "Funny. I was about to ask you the same thing."

Bailey shook her head. "The last thing I want is you dead." And she meant it.

He stared her, those ice-gray eyes seemingly going right through her. "Get inside," he ordered. "You might not value your life, but I'd prefer you stay alive so I can figure out who the hell you are."

She debated it, but in the end she couldn't dismiss the part about bullets going through glass. Yes, despite his comment that he preferred her alive, Jackson Malone might indeed have murder on his mind, but right now Bailey felt safer with him than she did with the ski-masked intruder. She only hoped she didn't regret trusting her instincts. She certainly didn't have a good track record in that department.

Bailey stepped out of the sunroom and into the main part of the house, and Jackson immediately closed the double doors and locked them. He pressed some numbers on a security system keypad, and then stepped in front of her to prevent her from going any farther.

"We'll wait here," he insisted.

Here was a casual living room with a butter-colored sofa. Floral chairs. A fireplace. There were toys in a basket on the hardwood floors.

That caused her breath to catch.

"Who's the intruder?" Jackson asked her, checking the phone again.

Bailey pulled her attention from the toys and that phone so she could shake her head. "I don't know, but maybe he came here to kidnap the baby."

"Funny, I was thinking the same thing about you," Jackson mumbled, making it sound like profanity. He shoved the gun into the back waist of his pants, crossed the room, pressed some buttons, and a bar opened from the wall. He poured himself a glass of something from a cut crystal decanter, tilted back his head and took the shot in one gulp.

"You have someone after the intruder?" she asked. "Someone who can stop him from getting inside?"

"I do. And my son has been taken to a panic room where no one can get to him. We've called the sheriff, and he's on the way. Now, what does the intruder want?"

Because her legs felt shaky, Bailey stepped to the side so she could lean against the wall. "I don't know."

"Then guess," he demanded. "And while you're guessing, try to figure out how this intruder could be linked to you."

"To *me?*"

"You," he verified.

He walked back to her and got close. Probably to violate her personal space and make her feel uncomfortable.

It worked.

Everything about him, from his clothes to his scent, to the liquor on his breath, screamed expensive, but that look he was giving her was from a powerful man who knew how to play down-and-dirty.

An attractive man, she reluctantly admitted to herself.

That's the first thing Bailey had noticed about him when she saw his photo in the newspapers. With his perfectly cut, but a little too-long hair, Jackson Malone looked like a bad boy rocker turned billionaire. He was drop-dead handsome, and despite the lousy circumstances and her personal feelings about him, her opinion about his looks didn't change. He was the kind of man women noticed, and she apparently wasn't exempt from that.

He glanced at her jeans pocket. "Why did you ask me about the two women in the photos?"

It was a simple question; and unlike many questions, Bailey actually knew the answer to this one, but she had to debate how much to tell him. She could just come clean about everything. That could cause him to gather up his soon-to-be adopted son and go deep into hiding, where he could keep the baby away from her.

Bailey wouldn't blame him for that.

But she couldn't risk Jackson leaving with the baby. She had to know the truth.

"Four months ago, when those men stormed into the hospital and took everyone hostage, I was in recovery. I'd just had a C-section." Bailey had to take a deep breath. She didn't remember much about that afternoon, and what she did remember wasn't good. Just blips on her mental radar. "I didn't know at the time, but the gunmen wanted to kill me."

"Because they thought you could identify them," he supplied. "I read about that."

She nodded. She'd read all about it, too—after the fact. "Apparently, the two gunmen tried to break into the hospital lab the day before, and they thought I'd seen them without their masks. I might have," she admitted.

"You don't remember?" he questioned.

"No. I was there for some pre-op tests, and my mind was on the baby I was going to have. But they didn't know that. They thought I was a threat. So they found out who I was and made a bogus call for me to come to the hospital for a bogus appointment. But I was already at the hospital because my labor started early."

He checked the phone monitor again. "Why didn't the gunmen just go into the recovery room after you?"

Bailey heard the question, but she had to know what was going on. Jackson kept looking at the phone, but he was giving her no clues as to what was happening. "Where's the intruder?"

"Still at the rear of the property. My men are closing in on him. Now, back to the question. Why didn't the gunmen go into recovery after you?"

"Because someone hid me, and my baby. I don't know the person who did that, but I think it might be one of the two women in those photos. Both of them worked at the hospital at the time of the hostage incident."

He made an impatient circling motion with his finger when she stopped. "Keep going."

"The woman told me she had to take my son because the gunmen might hurt him." Bailey had to pause again when she relived those last moments with her baby. "She took him and disappeared. I've been looking for him ever since, but I think someone doesn't want me to find him. There have been three attempts on my life."

Jackson made a sound of mild interest. "I read the gunmen are dead now, and the person who hired them is in prison."

She nodded. "But I'm pretty sure someone has continued to follow me. I don't know if it has anything to do with my missing son, or if it's just someone who wants to do a news story. Some of the former hostages have been hounded by reporters."

No sound of mild interest this time. He groaned, a deep rumbling in his throat, and cursed. "Still, someone tried to kill you, but you decided to come here anyway?"

"Those attempts on my life have nothing to do with this visit." She couldn't say it fast enough. "It's been days, weeks even, since anyone has followed me. That's why it was time for this visit. I thought I should come here today…."

"Say it," Jackson demanded when she stopped.

Bailey wasn't sure she could. She'd searched for so long, and it was bittersweet to think she might be this close and still be so far away from having the life she'd planned.

"I thought if I could see the child you're adopting," she whispered, "that I would know if he was—well—*mine*."

There it was. She'd just let him know that Caden James Malone could be the child who had been stolen from her.

And in Jackson's mind that meant she was the enemy.

She'd read all about him. The ruthless business practices, the endless string of properties and businesses he'd acquired, often through hostile takeovers. His failed marriage in his early twenties to a woman who'd turned out to be a gold-digging opportunist. Rumors were, the sour relationship had embarrassed him and his family and had cost him millions. And it had also caused him to vow to stay single for the rest of his life.

Obviously, that vow hadn't extended to fatherhood.

Bailey had poured over every article she could find, and it seemed as if, more than the money and his billion-dollar portfolio, the one thing Jackson Malone wanted most was children.

Now he had one.

And God knows what he would do to hang on to the baby.

"Do you have any proof?" he asked. There was pure skepticism in his tone.

"Some. I've researched all the adopted baby boys who were born in Texas on his birthday, and Caden is the only one I haven't been able to exclude."

He gave her a flat look. "Who says your son was adopted? He could have been taken to another state, or across the border. His adoption could have been illegal. Or maybe there was no adoption at all."

Yes. And that possibility had caused her many sleepless nights. Not knowing what had happened was the worst.

"I have my son's DNA," she continued. "I got it from the umbilical cord that had been saved after his delivery. The police kept that quiet so no one in the media would report it. They wanted to be able to use it when and if they found a baby matching my son's description. But the police also gave me a copy of those test results, and I was hoping you'd let me compare that DNA to the baby you're about to adopt."

His right eyebrow lifted, and he gave her a cold, hard stare to let her know that wasn't going to happen anytime soon.

"It's best for all of us if we know the truth," Bailey said, still trying.

"Really?" he challenged. "Here's what I do know." But a sound cut off whatever he'd been about to say.

It was a loud bang.

A gunshot.

Jackson's attention went straight to the phone, but he turned the screen so that she couldn't see.

"Because you came here today, you might have endangered my son," he continued, with his gaze fastened to the screen. "If what you've told me is true, someone could still be trying to kill you. So why the hell would you want to involve an innocent child in all of this?"

Her eyes burned, and Bailey tried to blink back the tears. She wasn't quite successful. "Because I don't think anyone is still trying to kill me. Besides, I had to know if he's my son."

"And then what?" Jackson snapped. He glared at her.

That was the hardest question of all, because she couldn't just walk away until she'd learned the truth.

She swallowed hard. Even if Caden was indeed her son, Jackson Malone wasn't just going to let her claim him. He no doubt approached fatherhood like he did his business, and that meant she was in another fight for her life.

"Caden's adoption is legal," Jackson concluded. "No one stole him from you. His birth mother is an unmarried college student from Austin who couldn't raise him, so she contacted a private adoption agency after he was born."

That was info that Bailey hadn't been able to uncover. But it didn't mean it was true. Maybe it was a story concocted by the woman who'd stolen Bailey's newborn.

His phone buzzed, and Jackson glanced down at the screen. He pulled in a deep breath and used the device to make a call. "Well?" he said to the person who answered.

Since this was likely about the intruder, Bailey tried to listen, but she couldn't hear the explanation that Jackson was getting. She held her breath, waiting.

"My men have the intruder," Jackson relayed to her when he hung up.

Relief flooded through her. "He's alive?"

"For the moment. He was wounded when he tried to run. That was the shot we heard."

But he was still alive. Bailey went to Jackson and caught onto his arm. "Have your men question him. Find out why he was here. You'll learn that he didn't come here because of me. He's probably a would-be kidnapper after the baby."

"The sheriff just arrived," Jackson said, not addressing anything she said. He stared at the grip she had on his arm, and didn't continue until Bailey drew back her hand. "And here's what I'm offering. You have two choices. You can leave now and look elsewhere for your missing baby. That includes you never attempting to contact me or my son again."

Her relief over the intruder's capture was short-lived. Bailey shook her head. "But don't you want to know the truth?"

Jackson shrugged. "I already know the truth, and

Caden is not yours. He's mine. Leave now, and someone on my staff will drive you back to San Antonio."

She couldn't leave. She might be just a room away from her baby.

"And if I refuse to leave?" Bailey challenged.

Another shrug. "Simple. The sheriff will arrest you for trespassing and take you to jail. Your choice, Miss Hodges. Which will it be?"

Chapter Three

Jackson rarely bluffed, but that's exactly what he was doing now.

Part of him, the paternal part, wanted this woman as far away from Caden as possible. He didn't want to believe a word she was saying. He wanted to dismiss those photos she carried around like emotional baggage.

But he couldn't.

He wasn't the type of man to live in denial.

"Okay," Bailey said. She nodded, drew in a long breath. "Have me arrested, but I'll pay the fine, or whatever, and keep coming back. I'm not going away. I *will* learn the truth."

So his bluff had failed. She hadn't backed down on her story. Still, that didn't mean she was Caden's birth mother. It didn't mean anything other than she was a woman who didn't give up easily.

Well, she'd met her match, because he didn't give up at all. *Ever.*

He checked the phone to see the progress going on outside. His men still had the intruder pinned down, and he could see the sheriff and his deputies approaching the ski-masked man.

Jackson wanted to be out there. He wanted to be the

one who got answers from this SOB who had dared to break in to the estate. But he had to stay put. He certainly didn't want to leave Bailey in the house with Caden. The first thing she would do is go look for the baby. She wouldn't find him, but he didn't want his staff to have to deal with containing her.

In the distance, he could hear the siren of an approaching ambulance. It wouldn't be long before the sheriff came inside to give him an update. By then, Jackson had to decide what to do about the brunette in front of him.

"If this is some kind of scam," he said to her, "I'll destroy you." Best to put that out there right up front. He might have toned down his ruthlessness, but he'd resort to a few old habits if this woman was out for money.

"It's no scam. I just want to know if he's my son."

Jackson moved closer to her again, because he knew it made her nervous. The last time he'd gotten in her face, her bottom lip had trembled. He didn't get any satisfaction at the idea of frightening her, but it might be the fastest way to get to the so-called truth that she claimed she wanted.

He slid his gaze over her. All over her. And he mentally pulled back a little when he felt that punch of attraction again. Hell. Hadn't his past taught him anything? He couldn't live his life thinking below the belt.

"Caden doesn't look like you," he pointed out.

She touched her hand to her short, spiky hair. Yep, she was trembling all right. "This isn't my natural color. I dyed it after the attempts on my life. I have black hair, like yours."

Like Caden's.

But he kept that to himself.

"What color are his eyes?" she asked. Despite the trembling, she no longer seemed afraid. She seemed— well—*hopeful*.

"Blue."

Similar to Bailey's.

But many people had blue eyes, he reminded himself. Not that shade though. When he'd first seen her eyes, he'd thought they were memorable. And they were. Because they were a close match to Caden's.

"Blue," she repeated, smiling. The smile quickly faded though. "You said he was safe? Are you sure?"

"Positive." To prove it to himself, he used his phone to scan through the security cameras, and he zoomed in on the panic room. Caden was there, still asleep. His nanny, Tracy Collier, was holding him.

"May I see him?" Bailey's voice had so much breath in it that it hardly had any sound. Also, there was that hopefulness in it again.

But Jackson didn't show her the images on his screen, and he wouldn't. Not until he'd done some investigating, and even then it might not happen.

He used the phone to call Evan again, and, as expected, his business manager answered on the first ring.

"Is everyone okay?" Evan immediately asked.

Jackson settled for saying, "They caught the intruder."

"Yes. I was watching the security feed, but I'm on my way out to the estate now. I figured you might need some help."

"I do, as a matter of fact." His gaze met Bailey's, and he didn't think it was his imagination that she was holding her breath. "I need you to get the contact info for Caden's birth mother."

Evan didn't answer for several moments. "Are you sure?"

"Positive."

A lot of money had gone into that private adoption. Well over a million dollars. The attorney had said it was to expedite the process and to pay the birth mother's expenses, both medical and the cost of her return to college. Jackson hoped that was all the money had been used for, and that it wasn't part of some illegal process.

"Anything else?" Evan asked.

Jackson looked at Bailey again. "Yes. Get me a detailed report of the hostage incident at the maternity hospital. I want everything the cops have, including info on employees they might have suspected in the disappearance of Bailey Hodges's newborn."

Evan made a sound of disapproval. "That sounds like a messy can of worms you're opening, Jackson."

Yes, it was, but this particular can was already open, and the proof was standing in front of him.

"I have the women's names," Bailey volunteered the moment he ended the call with Evan. "And I've ruled out everyone else who was on the maternity ward that afternoon. Well, hopefully. There's always the possibility that the woman who took my son wasn't on any official records. She could have come in with the gunmen."

And if that were true, then there'd be no way to trace her. That would mean no definitive answer for Bailey. That, in turn, meant she wouldn't make a hasty exit out of his life. The fastest way to end this was to figure out what had happened to her son.

"Give me the photos," he instructed.

She pulled the folded sheet of paper from her jeans and handed it to him. But not without touching him. Her fingers brushed his. She was still trembling.

Hell.

He didn't want her fear and emotions—or his reaction to them—to have any part in this. He wanted a cool detachment between Bailey and himself while he helped her, and himself. But that zing of heat didn't equal anything cool. Jackson was betting the detachment wouldn't go far, either. And that meant he had to do something about it.

Bailey jerked back her hand as if he'd scalded her, and she dodged his gaze when she spoke. "The first woman is Shannon Wright, an RN who was on the fourth floor of the hospital that day, but no one remembers seeing her after the gunmen arrived. She claims she hid."

It was possible Shannon Wright was telling the truth—hiding would be the logical thing to do—but Bailey was right to suspect her.

"The second one is Robin Russo. She works in records in the administration section. The other floors of the hospital were evacuated after the gunmen arrived in the maternity ward, and someone saw Robin leave her office, but no one, including the police, actually saw her leave the building."

Jackson gave that some thought. "You have a motive for either of these women?"

She shook her head. "Well, unless they got money from selling my baby to someone."

And that was something Jackson couldn't rule out—yet—but he would.

"What about your son's father?" Jackson asked. "Maybe he's the one who had your son taken?"

Another headshake. "My baby's father broke off things with me when I told him I was pregnant. He took a job in Europe, and I haven't heard from him, other than an email to remind me that he wanted nothing to do with the child."

Jackson tried not to have any visible reaction to that, but her story only made him feel more sympathy for her. And empathy, because of his own bad relationship. He had to keep his distance from her, because empathy and attraction were a lethal combination.

"If I find out you're lying about any of this…" he reiterated.

"I know. You'll destroy me. And if I find out you knowingly stole my son, all your money and power won't stop me from coming after you."

He almost smiled. Almost. Considering her predicament, she still had some fight in her.

That wouldn't mix well with the attraction, either.

"The sheriff will come inside any minute," he reminded her and himself. "If you're here, he'll want to know why. Are you prepared to answer his questions?"

Jackson didn't want her out of his sight, but he also didn't want to risk her being underfoot. He would have her followed when she left, so he could keep tabs on her until he had more information about her and her missing child.

"I'm prepared. Well, as prepared as I can be. The last time I was in protective custody, I was nearly killed." She paused. "I suppose it could happen again. That's the reason I've avoided the cops, but I'm too close to turn back now."

It was what he expected her to say. So he had to do whatever was necessary to speed up this process and get her out of his and Caden's lives.

"May I see Caden?" she asked.

"No." Jackson didn't even have to think about it.

She nodded, and paused as if she might challenge that. But she didn't.

The intercom system made a slight buzzing sound. A moment later, his household manager, Steven Perez, spoke through the tiny speaker built into the wall. "Sheriff Gentry is out front waiting for the ambulance. He says once he has the man on the way to the hospital, he wants to speak to Bailey Hodges if she's still on the grounds."

The color drained from Bailey's face. "How did the sheriff know I was here? And how did he know my name? Did you tell him?" She still didn't look ready to bolt, but it was possible she might faint. Or hyperventilate.

"No. I didn't tell him your name, but you can trust the sheriff," Jackson told her. "I've known Alden Gentry my whole life, and he wouldn't do anything illegal."

Still, Bailey shook her head…and then she tried to grab his gun. He snagged her wrist, but she tried to get the weapon with her left hand.

Jackson finally just caught onto her shoulders and put her against the wall. Body-to-body. Not the brightest idea he'd ever had, but it stopped her.

"Please," she said, her warm breath brushing against his mouth at the same time her breasts pressed against his chest.

That "please" wouldn't work, but Jackson knew it wasn't a good idea to keep touching her like this.

"Why does Sheriff Gentry want to see Miss Hodges?" Jackson asked, directing his question to the intercom so that Steven would hear him.

"Because she might be involved with the intruder," Steven answered at the same moment that Bailey issued a denial.

"I had nothing to do with this," she insisted.

"Not according to the sheriff," Steven contradicted. "When Sheriff Gentry approached the man, he said Bailey Hodges brought him to the estate with her."

Her breath was gusting even harder now, and she frantically shook her head. She also struggled to break free of his grip. But Jackson held on.

"Did the intruder say why she brought him here?" Jackson asked.

"He did." Steven paused again. "He claims Bailey Hodges paid him to kill you."

Chapter Four

Bailey made a sound of outrage, but she wasn't able to speak. She could only grab onto Jackson and shake her head, denying the intruder's accusation.

He claims Bailey Hodges paid him to kill you.

"I didn't," she finally managed to say. "I swear, I didn't hire anyone to do anything."

But she didn't even wait for Jackson's response. Why should he believe her? She'd lied her way into his home and had then tried to escape when he confronted her.

Mercy.

She was so desperate to find her son that all her desperation must have made her seem insane. And maybe she was. She certainly hadn't slept through the night since this entire nightmare had started four months ago. Jackson might have her arrested or hauled off to the loony bin.

This visit could cost her everything. And that cut through her heart.

The pain and the frustration slammed through her, and Bailey felt her legs turn boneless. Much to her disgust, she even started to cry. She would have no doubt fallen to the floor if Jackson still hadn't had her in his grip.

"I didn't," she pled, though the words barely had any sound. Her throat had clamped shut, and the tears were streaming down her cheeks.

With Jackson's body still holding her in place against the wall, steadying her, he used his left hand to lift her chin. Bailey didn't want to make eye contact, because she figured she knew what she would see there on his face: his determination to have her arrested.

But his ice-gray eyes combed over her for what seemed an eternity.

And then he cursed.

He kept on cursing when he let go of her and stepped back.

"Leave us," Jackson told the man who had rushed in and relayed what the sheriff had said. "Tell Sheriff Gentry the intruder is lying. Miss Hodges is a guest in my home and didn't hire anyone to kill me."

The man looked suspiciously at Bailey. "You're sure, sir?"

Jackson hesitated. "I'm sure." But he sounded far from convinced of her innocence. "I want to speak to the intruder before the ambulance takes him to the hospital. Let the sheriff know that."

When the man hurried out, Bailey shook her head again, not understanding. And Jackson didn't explain. He latched on to her arm and practically dragged her to the sofa, where he had her sit. He rummaged through his pocket, extracted a handkerchief and thrust it into her hand.

"Wipe your eyes," he snarled.

She did, but the tears continued to come. Bailey stared up at him, blinking back more tears. And waiting. Jackson scrubbed his hand over his face, groaned and paced.

"Convince me," he finally said. "Tell me why I should believe that you didn't hire someone to come here and kill me."

Bailey certainly hadn't expected this gift. And it was definitely a gift. It was possible Jackson had called off the sheriff simply because he didn't want the authorities questioning him about Caden or the adoption. If the sheriff took her into custody, there would certainly be questions.

Did that mean Jackson had something to hide about the adoption?

Possibly. Or it could be a simple matter of his wanting to get to the bottom of this himself. That was certainly what she wanted. Bailey had been hiding in fear for her life for four months, unable to trust anyone, and seemingly not getting any closer to finding her baby. Maybe, just maybe, this was her first positive step in the right direction.

Or it could be a fatal mistake.

"My medical records prove I had a child," she said, not really knowing where to start. Jackson continued to pace. "And you know from police reports that my newborn went missing. A woman took him."

He stopped, and that icy gaze snapped onto her. "One of the women in those photos? Shannon Wright or Robin Russo?"

She nodded, surprised that he could recall the names. He'd barely glanced at the photos when she had shown them to him earlier. "Was one of them involved in your son's adoption?"

"No." And he didn't hesitate. "I've never seen either of them before."

Bailey believed him. Maybe because he believed that she hadn't hired that intruder. Of course, this could all be an act, but the truth was, she could be under the same roof as her son. That was worth any risk.

"Those photos aren't proof that Caden is your missing baby," Jackson pointed out.

"No." Bailey wiped away the last of the tears and gathered her resolve. "But I could have DNA proof."

His stare narrowed, and she could have sworn it took on a lethal edge. Now here was the Jackson Malone she'd read about.

Ruthless. Dangerous. Intimidating.

"Remember, I told you my son's umbilical cord was stored right after he was born," Bailey explained. "It's there at the San Antonio Maternity Hospital storage facility. The police worked up a DNA profile from it, and you could compare it to Caden's."

He blinked. That was his only change of expression, but Bailey thought he was both shocked and terrified about the possible outcome.

She understood completely.

If the DNA didn't match, then this would be a painful dead end for her to accept. She wouldn't stop looking for her baby. She would *never* stop. But as long as she didn't feel safe trusting the police, that would slow down her search. Eventually, she would run out of money. And resources. God knows what she would do then.

But a DNA match could at least let her know that her baby was alive and safe. Later, she could deal with getting him back. Right now, the "alive and safe" part was the most critical.

"The police have the DNA profile," she continued after trying to clear her throat. "I also have a copy in a safe deposit box."

"A profile that could have been doctored," Jackson snapped.

Bailey nodded, readily accepting his doubts about that. "But then, of course, there's me. My own DNA. You can do what's called a maternity study and see if Caden's DNA matches mine."

Jackson squeezed his eyes shut a moment and then started to pace again. At least that's what she thought he was doing, but then he headed out of the room.

"I want to talk to the intruder," he let her know.

Bailey jumped from the sofa and hurried after him. "So do I. But I also want to know the truth about Caden."

He stopped and whirled around so fast that she plowed right into him. Suddenly, his arms were all around her, embracing her. Well, almost. Just as quickly, he pushed her away, but not before she caught his scent. Yet something else about him that smelled expensive.

"No more talk about Caden, especially not to an armed man who trespassed onto the grounds of my estate," Jackson warned. "Something is happening, something dangerous, and I want to keep my son out of it."

Bailey opened her mouth to try to change his mind, but she couldn't. He was right. Something dangerous was indeed happening, and she had to try to stop the immediate danger first. That had to be her priority. Then she could press Jackson for the DNA test.

"We're not on opposites sides of this," she tried to

tell him. "We both want Caden safe. And we both want the truth about what's going on."

"Oh, we're on opposite sides all right," he snarled.

Jackson didn't wait for her to respond to that. He went through the foyer and to the front door. He shot her a warning glance before he stepped onto the porch. That warning was no doubt a reminder for her to stay quiet about the adoption.

The front lawn was nothing short of chaos. The decorators were still there, all standing away from the sheriff, two deputies and several men that she suspected were Jackson's employees. There were at least a dozen of them milling around, shouting out orders, talking on their phones. In the distance, Bailey could hear the sound of the ambulance siren.

Lying facedown on the ground in the center was a man wearing military-style camouflaged clothing. There was a bloody gash on his sleeve where he had no doubt been shot, and next to him was a black ski mask.

He lifted his head and looked up at her. And despite the look of pain on his face, his mouth bent into an oily smile.

"You recognize him?" Jackson asked.

"No." In her four-month-long ordeal, she'd never seen him.

Bailey wanted to demand to know why he had accused her of trying to kill Jackson, or why he had aimed that smile at her, but she decided to heed Jackson's warning and approach all of this with caution. She certainly didn't want to give the injured man any more information.

"What's his name?" Bailey asked, hoping that someone would be able to answer.

The tall, lanky sheriff looked at her. "He hasn't volunteered that yet." Then he raised an eyebrow when he turned his attention to Jackson. "You're sure I don't need to take her into custody?" the sheriff asked.

But Jackson didn't answer the question. He stared at the wounded intruder. "Has he said anything else about why he's here at the estate?"

The sheriff shook his head, but his eyebrow stayed cocked. "You do know I'll need answers—about her, about this guy on the ground and about any- and everything else that might be going on around here," the sheriff said, volleying his cop's gaze between Jackson and her.

"Yes," was all Jackson had time to say before someone shouted his name.

Bailey spotted the sandy-haired man making his way across the lawn toward them, and this time it was someone she did recognize. From his photos, that is. She'd seen articles about him in the newspaper archives that she'd researched when she had checked Jackson out. This was Evan Young, Jackson's business manager, and in fact, he'd been in the photo that had started her suspicions about Caden being her missing baby.

The San Antonio paper had printed a photo of Jackson coming out of family court after filing the successful adoption petition. He'd held a blanket-wrapped Caden in his arms, and behind him in that photo was Evan. All she had been able to see of the baby was his dark hair, and that had planted the seed that he could be hers.

"You should be inside," Evan said, and he tried to catch on to Jackson's arm.

Jackson threw off his grip. "In a minute." He went closer to the intruder and stooped down.

Because of the approaching siren from the ambulance, Bailey couldn't hear what Jackson said to the man, but it erased any trace of that slimy smile he'd given her. She walked toward them, hoping to hear the truth about why he was there, but Evan stopped her.

"I wouldn't advise that," he shouted over the howl of the siren. "The man is obviously dangerous."

Their gazes connected, and while Evan's tone seemed to indicate that he was concerned about her safety, she saw no such concern in his eyes. However, she did keep her distance because the ambulance pulled to a stop between Jackson and her. Since Evan was already tugging her in that direction, she stepped onto the porch with him.

The siren stopped and the medics jumped from the ambulance.

"Are you responsible for any of this?" Evan asked her.

"No. I have no reason to want Jackson harmed."

"Right," he mumbled.

She wasn't surprised he was suspicious. After all, Jackson had asked Evan to run some kind of background check on her so the man knew his boss had suspicions of his own. Plus, the intruder had lied about her hiring him.

"Jackson's going through a difficult time right now," Evan continued. "Did he tell you that someone sent him a threatening letter this morning?"

"He mentioned it," Bailey said, recalling Jackson's

question to her in the foyer. "He said he faxed a copy to SAPD."

"Really?" Evan pulled back his shoulders. "Jackson doesn't usually involve the police in his personal matters."

But this was more than personal—it was a safety issue that might spill over to Caden. "Just what kind of threat was it?"

Evan hesitated so long, she wasn't sure he was going to answer her. "It said 'Jackson Malone, I won't forgive and forget. Watch your back.' Someone left it outside his San Antonio office, but two others were left on his car when it was parked in the underground garage at work."

Bailey shook her head. "Maybe it's related to his business?"

He made a sound deep within his throat that hinted it might be related to her. But how could it be? If the person or persons who wanted her dead also wanted to silence her for something connected to the hostage situation, then why go after Jackson?

"The bottom line is that it isn't a good time for you to be here," Evan warned.

"Maybe not," Jackson interrupted. He had obviously overheard what his business manager had said. "But she's staying until I clear up some things."

Bailey was thankful that he might actually believe she was innocent, but she didn't think Jackson was extending any invitations for her to see Caden. "What did you say to the intruder?"

"I told him I would bury him if he didn't tell me the truth." Jackson said it calmly, but there was nothing calm about his demeanor.

"Did he tell you who he is?" Bailey pressed.

"No. But I suspect he's some kind of hired gun. He doesn't seem smart enough to pull a stunt like this on his own. When the sheriff runs his prints, I'm betting we'll know a lot more about him." He turned to Evan. "Why are you here?"

Evan shrugged, as if the answer were obvious. "First the threatening letter. Then Bailey's arrival. I thought you could use a little backup."

The muscles in Jackson's jaw stirred, but he kept his attention fastened to the injured man the medics were loading into the ambulance.

"In addition to getting me the info on Caden's birth mother, there is something you can do," he said to Evan as the ambulance drove away. The sheriff and one of the deputies followed along right behind it. "There are two women who were at the hospital during the hostage situation. Shannon Wright and Robin Russo. I need you to dig deep and see if one of them possibly took Bailey's son."

"Considering they were connected to the hostages and investigation that followed, I'm sure the cops have already done this," Evan quickly pointed out.

"Do it again." And it was definitely an order. "While you're at it, I want another thorough background check on Ryan Cassaine." Now Jackson looked at her. "He's the adoption attorney I used."

That sent her heart racing again. Did that mean Jackson was at least allowing for the possibility that Caden was her son?

"Why are you doing this?" she heard herself whisper. "Why are you willing to help me?"

"I'm not," Jackson quickly clarified. "I want the truth

so I can get you out of my life. I don't believe Caden is yours. I think you're so desperate to find your child that you're willing to latch on to mine."

That stung more than she thought. Probably because she had started to feel this weird camaraderie between them. And the equally weird attraction. But Bailey just realized that Jackson had put her in her place.

"You're not going to have her taken into custody for questioning?" Evan demanded.

Again, Jackson hesitated. "No. Not until I have the answers I want."

Answers the intruder might provide. But there was another way to settle one aspect of this baby issue once and for all. "You can do the test to compare Caden's DNA to mine," she reminded Jackson in a whisper. However, her lowered voice failed because Evan obviously heard her anyway.

"A DNA test is a bad idea," Evan instantly responded. Again, he tried to take Jackson aside, but Jackson held his ground. "Consult your legal department. I doubt one of those highly paid lawyers will tell you to consent to anything this woman wants."

Jackson stayed quiet a moment. "Probably not." Another pause. "But arrange for the test anyway." He went inside with Evan right on his heels.

Had she just heard Jackson correctly? Was he really going to allow the test, or was this some kind of trick to placate her?

"You can't do this," Evan insisted. "She could be a scam artist."

"Then the test will prove that."

Still stunned about Jackson's possible cooperation, Bailey continued to follow the men so she could listen.

"But it could prove...*other* things," Evan said, lowering his voice to a near whisper. Bailey heard him anyway.

Yes, it could prove the adoption was illegal. Jackson could lose custody of the baby he was trying to adopt.

Jackson had been practically iron-jawed during this conversation, and for that matter, the crazy events of the day, but she saw the flash of pain on his face. Pain she understood. He wasn't just Caden's soon-to-be adoptive father, he obviously loved the child, and ironically, if Caden was her son, Jackson had spent more time with the baby than she had.

Bailey hadn't even gotten to hold him.

"Do the background checks on the adoption attorney and the two women from the hospital," Jackson continued, talking to Evan. The pain was gone, and the iron-dragon persona was back in place. "Get that DNA test here today."

Evan's chin came up, and there was fire in his eyes. "And if I object?"

"You won't," Jackson simply answered, and he walked away.

Obviously fuming now, Evan started to leave, but then he turned to her. He pointed his finger in her face. "So help me, if you do anything to hurt Jackson or the baby, I'll make sure you're locked up for the rest of your life."

That was yet another surprise. Here, Jackson had just butted heads with the man, and yet Evan was protecting his boss. And his boss's son. Part of her appreciated that, because Bailey was worried that all of them might need protection before this was over.

"Your business manager obviously doesn't want me here," Bailey mumbled as Evan walked away.

"Neither do I," Jackson mumbled back. He looked over his shoulder at her, his gaze searing right into her.

That seemed to be her cue to leave. But Bailey didn't want to do that until she had tried one more time. "May I see Caden?"

Jackson turned so quickly that it startled her. Bailey jumped back, overbalancing herself, just as he caught her. Unlike before though when he had stopped her from falling, the grip he had on her arms felt punishing.

"No," he answered, though she had no idea how he could speak with his jaw clench that tight.

It seemed as if he wanted to say something else, but he shook his head and tightened his grip even more.

She winced, made a small sound of pain, and just like that, he jerked back. He stared at his hands a moment and then gently pushed up her sleeve.

"I'm sorry," he whispered.

Bailey looked down at her forearm. "You didn't bruise me," she let him know.

"But I came damn close." He groaned and rolled his eyes toward the ornate ceiling. "There was a time in my life when I would have intimidated you into leaving."

She nodded. "There was a time in my life when I would have been intimidated. Not now, though. Not with the possibility of finding my baby at stake."

Bailey inched closer and reached out. Mercy, she was afraid to touch him. Not because she didn't want to do exactly that, but because she knew that touching was the last thing they needed. Their minds were both racing with the possibilities of her and Caden's DNA.

And racing with other things, too.

For some reason, being around Jackson reminded her that it had been well over a year since a man had touched her in any kind of way. Over a year since she had been in a man's arms. A year since she'd felt that trickle of heat in her body.

Jackson was the wrong man to make her feel any kind of trickle. But she couldn't seem to convince herself of that.

She put her hand on his arm, in about the same spot where he had gripped her. But instead of pouring her frustration and anger into that grip, she traced her finger slightly down his arm. Hopefully, a gesture to soothe him.

He probably thought she was sucking up to him, but Bailey didn't care. She didn't want to make an enemy of this man.

Even if they felt like enemies.

After all, he could have her son, and he could be keeping the baby from her.

"So what do we do?" she asked.

He blew out a long breath and checked his watch. "I need to bring Caden out of the panic room. He's probably up from his nap now, and I don't want him frightened by the strange surroundings."

Again, her heart latched right on to that as a possible opening. Even though it didn't make sense, Bailey thought if she saw the baby that she would immediately know if he was hers or not.

"No," Jackson said, and he realized he was staring

at her. "I can't let you see him because, quite frankly, I don't trust you."

She nodded, accepting that. Bailey didn't fully trust him, either. "You won't try to hide Caden so I can't get to him?"

Jackson's hesitation didn't help the tightness in her chest. "I agreed to the DNA test, and I'll have it done. But that's only because I don't believe he's yours. Think this through," he said, pulling away from her. "Someone stole your child. So why would that person risk placing the baby up for adoption?"

Bailey had an answer, only because this had constantly been on her mind. "Two possible reasons—as long as the woman has the baby with her, he, and therefore she, could be linked to the hostage situation. Plus, she kidnapped my son. Her intentions might have been good at the time. She might truly have wanted to save my baby's life. But when she didn't return him, she became a kidnapper and therefore a felon."

He continued to study her. "And the second reason?"

"Money. I read this was a private adoption. Money no doubt changed hands."

"It did. But I paid it through an attorney to Caden's birth mother, who was a college student."

Bailey gave that some thought. It could have been the college student in that hospital room with her. Bailey had no idea who had walked out with her baby that day. "Does this student have any DNA proof that the child is hers?"

"No. But then neither do you." Jackson tossed his comment right back at her.

"Not yet anyway."

She instantly regretted that snap, because it put some fire in his eyes. Fire that she didn't want there.

"You can wait in the guesthouse until Evan returns with the DNA kit." His voice was cool now. Detached. With just that arrogance and suspicion she'd encountered when he first walked down the stairs and confronted her. "I'll have one of the servants show you the way."

Jackson reached for the phone on an end table, but he didn't get a chance to pick it up. His own cell rang, and after glancing at the caller ID screen, he answered it right away.

"Sheriff," he greeted. "Please tell me you learned the identity of the intruder."

Bailey moved closer, hoping to hear the sheriff's response. This could be big. If she knew the man's name, then maybe she could learn who had hired him.

"What?" Jackson asked. Not exactly the tone of a question. More like stunned anger. "How the hell did that happen?"

Alarmed, Bailey went even closer, but she still couldn't hear what the lawman was saying. *My God, what had gone wrong now?* Had the man managed to escape? If so, he might double back and try to break into the estate again.

He might endanger Caden.

Even if the baby wasn't hers, she didn't want him in danger. It had been a horrible mistake coming here, she admitted to herself, again.

Jackson slapped his phone shut, but he didn't say anything right away, despite the fact he obviously knew

Bailey was anxious to hear what the sheriff had just told him.

"Well?" she prompted. "The intruder got away?"

Jackson shook his head. "Worse."

Chapter Five

Jackson listened to Sheriff Gentry's latest account of his investigation, but it was hard to concentrate with Caden staring up at him with those big blue eyes.

It was morning. Caden's favorite time of the day, when he seemed to be full of energy and new discoveries. His son had just squealed with delight—though Jackson didn't know why—and now Caden seemed to be waiting for him to respond to that baby outburst. Jackson did. He gave the boy an exaggerated grin that caused Caden to grin back.

"You do know what this means?" the sheriff asked, his somber voice pouring through the speakerphone on Jackson's desk.

Jackson did know. The day before, he'd listened to every word of Sheriff Gentry's account of what had happened when the ambulance arrived at the hospital with the intruder. The minute the medics had taken the man out to usher him into the ER, someone fired shots.

Now Jackson was listening to the latest update: the shots had been fired from a long-range high-powered rifle. The intruder had been killed instantly. There were no signs of the killer or the weapon he used.

"This means it was probably a professional hit," the sheriff continued.

Yeah. Jackson had come to the same conclusion. "And still no ID on the intruder?"

"No, because the man had no fingerprints. I don't mean none were on file. The man had no prints, period. They'd been burnt off with acid or something. It looked like a sloppy job, but an amateur isn't likely to go that far to conceal his identity. Of course, we'll still try to do a DNA match from our database."

They might get lucky. *Might.* But Jackson had to accept that the intruder was a dead end, literally. Besides, those missing prints were the sign of yet another pro. A hired gun in his own right.

So why had he trespassed onto the estate?

"You want me to send a deputy out to your place?" the sheriff asked.

"No. I have enough security." He hoped. And while he was hoping, Jackson added that he hoped he could get all of this cleared up fast. The situation with the latest threatening letter. With the intruder.

And especially with Bailey.

He wanted to enjoy every moment of Caden's first Christmas; but here he was, worried to the bone that instead of a celebration, his son could be in danger.

"What about your houseguest?" the sheriff asked, as if reading Jackson's mind.

Of course, it wasn't anything as miraculous as mind-reading. In a small town like Copper Creek, secrets didn't stay secrets very long, and the sheriff or his deputies had interviewed some of Jackson's staff. Sheriff Gentry knew that Bailey had spent the night at the estate.

"I'm not sure about Bailey Hodges yet," Jackson settled for saying. "Have you made any connection between the intruder and her?"

"Zero. The dead man had a prepaid cell in his pocket, with only one number called, and it wasn't to Miss Hodges. It was to a woman, Shannon Wright."

Jackson froze for a moment. "Shannon Wright? The nurse who was at the San Antonio Maternity Hospital during the hostage situation?"

"Yeah. How'd you know that?" the sheriff asked.

"It wasn't a lucky guess. Bailey thinks this Shannon Wright is a possible suspect in her baby's disappearance."

"Interesting. I'll look into it." The sheriff paused. "Where exactly is Miss Hodges right now?"

"In the guest quarters, away from the main house." Jackson paused to reach for the stuffed toy horse that Caden was offering him. Of course, the moment he took it Caden wanted it back. This was a game that Jackson knew all too well, and it made him smile.

"Good," the sheriff concluded.

That grabbed Jackson's attention. "Good? Why?" Because he certainly didn't consider it a good thing. He wanted her away from the estate, and that would happen as soon as he got the results of the DNA swabs he'd taken from her the day before. Then he would get Bailey on her way, if the results were what he wanted.

And what Jackson wanted was proof that she wasn't Caden's biological mother.

If she was, well, that was a kettle of fish he'd deal with later. One thing was for certain, no matter what the results were, he wasn't just going to hand over the baby to her—or anyone else.

Caden was *his*.

"San Antonio PD wants to question Bailey again," Sheriff Gentry explained. "You do know she hasn't been cooperative with them since shortly after the hostage incident four months ago?"

"Yes. Because she claims someone tried to kill her while she was in protective custody."

"Someone did try, just a day after the hostage situation ended. SAPD thinks the attempts were made by the now-dead gunmen, but they aren't sure. No proof. Personally, it sounds as if she should be back in San Antonio, trying to work with the cops who are running that investigation. She doesn't need to be out here in Copper Creek."

The sheriff obviously didn't know that Bailey was looking into the matter of Caden's DNA. Of course, that left Jackson with something he couldn't explain.

Knowing what Bailey thought about Caden, why had he let her stay?

He mentally cursed. It was this damn camaraderie over the near-death experience they'd survived. Plus, the baby angle. He now understood all about a parent's love for a child, and he could see that Bailey was desperate for answers about her lost baby.

There was also the damn attraction. Jackson only hoped that it wasn't playing into this. On most days he didn't think below the belt, but for reasons he didn't want to explore, that seemed to be happening with Bailey. But his camaraderie and stupid testosterone weren't going to run wild here.

"My plan is to have her gone as soon as possible," Jackson assured Sheriff Gentry. As soon as he had those test results. "Let me know if you get anything else on the intruder or his killer."

The sheriff assured him that he would, and Jackson ended the call.

Despite everything that was now weighing heavily on his mind, Jackson pushed it all aside and got down on the thick quilt that he kept on his office floor. It was Caden's favorite spot, and when he placed the baby on his stomach, Caden immediately began to move his arms and legs, causing his denim overalls to slide against the quilt. Caden couldn't crawl, but he seemed to love attempting it.

The phone rang, but when he glanced at the caller ID he saw it was a client. A client who could wait. Jackson let it go to voicemail and continued his daddy time with Caden.

It was amazing how much he loved his son. Amazing even more that he was already thinking of adding another addition to his family. Maybe a daughter. Heck, he might even give up his investment company and adopt a whole houseful of kids. His thirst to add more and more millions to his billion dollar portfolio just wasn't there anymore.

There was a knock at the door and Jackson decided to ignore it as well. But then it opened, and he had no choice but to look up from Caden.

It was Bailey.

Jackson silently cursed. He'd instructed his staff to tell him if Bailey left the guest quarters.

He got to his feet, leaving Caden to play on the floor, and he did that not just because his son was having fun. Jackson also did it because his desk blocked Bailey from seeing the baby. *That wasn't being petty,* he assured himself. *It was simply sheltering Caden from a woman who could potentially be a threat.*

The intercom on his desk buzzed, and a moment later he heard his house manager's voice. "I'm sorry, sir," Steven Perez told him. "I just got the word that Miss Hodges is on the way to your office."

"She's here," Jackson let him know. "Instruct the staff to give me a faster heads-up if this happens again. I know we're not accustomed to these security measures, but I want everyone to do a better job."

"Of course, sir. Do you need me there?" In other words, did Jackson want Perez to have Bailey removed?

"I'll take care of it," Jackson insisted, and he pressed the button to end the transmission. He put his hands on his hips and stared at her, waiting.

Bailey certainly didn't look like a threat, standing there. She looked lost and scared. Hell. Jackson felt that need to console her again, but he resisted.

What he couldn't resist was noticing what she was wearing. The loose, casual red dress skimmed over her body and created an interesting contrast with her milky-white skin. It was a loaner dress no doubt, and probably belonged to someone on his staff, since Bailey hadn't arrived with a change of clothes, or even any toiletries.

"I'm sorry," Bailey said. "I just thought maybe you had an update on the dead intruder."

He did, but he didn't intend to discuss anything with her while Caden was in the room. Jackson hit the button on the intercom that would no doubt send the nanny hurrying to his office.

Caden squealed, the sound of happiness amplifying through the room.

Bailey gasped and put her hand to her heart. She

hurried toward his desk, toward the sound, but Jackson blocked her from racing behind it. Still, she came up on her toes and looked over his shoulder.

The sound she made would have melted a heart of stone. It was a painful mix of shock, joy and loss all rolled into one. Jackson looked deep into her eyes, to see if all that emotional mix would give him clues as to what she thinking. But she was only staring in awe at Caden.

"He's beautiful," she muttered, her voice as filled with emotion as her eyes suddenly were.

Did that mean she believed this was her son?

Jackson didn't ask her, and she didn't have time to volunteer. Tracy Collier, the nanny, came into the room. She stopped just in the doorway, probably trying to figure out what the heck was going on, but Jackson gave her a nod. That nod sent Tracy behind his desk, where she scooped up Caden into her arms.

"Tell Daddy bye-bye," Tracy prompted, kissing Caden on the cheek.

"D-d-d-d," Caden echoed.

It was Caden's new sound, something he'd been saying for several days, but each time Jackson heard it, he was reminded of just how much he loved his little boy.

"He's already trying to say 'daddy,'" Bailey mumbled. "That's early. All the books I read said that normally happens at six months, or sometimes even later." She kept her attention fastened to Caden until the nanny and he were out of sight. She likely would have followed them if Jackson hadn't caught hold of her.

"No," was all Jackson could manage to say. He

didn't want his son part of what would no doubt be an emotional encounter unless he had no other choice.

She blinked back tears and finally nodded. "He looks like me."

"He looks like a four-month-old baby," Jackson countered. But he couldn't dismiss that there might be a resemblance. With that added to the fact that someone had indeed stolen Bailey's son, he knew he had to start accepting that a DNA match was a possibility.

How much money would it take to make her go away?

Just the thought of it sounded ruthless and made him sick to his stomach. Like the old Jackson. But he rationalized that if Bailey could indeed be paid off, then she wasn't much of a mother anyway. So he would make the offer, and maybe, just maybe, it would be an offer she couldn't turn down.

He poured her a cup of coffee from the silver carafe on his desk and motioned for her to sit. She took the coffee, the cup rattling because of her shaky hands, but she didn't sit.

"When will Evan have the test results from the DNA swabs?" she asked.

"Maybe as early as this afternoon." For those results anyway.

Jackson had arranged for others that he wouldn't mention to Bailey or Evan. Old habits died hard, and Jackson had wanted some kind of backup for the tests.

She nodded again and took a sip of the coffee. At least she tried, but the shaking sloshed it out of the cup and onto her hand. Jackson took the cup from her and put it back on his desk.

"The sheriff just called," he told her. Best to use this

time to give her an update, rather than go back to the subject of Caden. He also checked her hand to make sure the hot coffee hadn't burnt her. "No identity yet on the dead intruder."

Bailey didn't do a good job of hiding her disappointment. "And the person who killed him?"

"Nothing yet on that, either. But the intruder did call Nurse Shannon Wright."

She took a deep breath and slowly drew back her hand. "Shannon," she repeated. "And does she have an explanation why a possible killer would have called her?"

"Not yet. The sheriff will look into it. But don't get your hopes up that Shannon is guilty of anything. The intruder accused you of hiring him, so he could have also made a call to Shannon to implicate her."

"Of course. I hadn't thought of that." She paused. "Thank you for letting me stay last night. I was a wreck. Still am," she added in a mumble.

He didn't doubt that. He wasn't feeling at ease either. "Who knew you were coming here to the estate?"

Bailey shook her head. "No one should have known. I used an alias when I applied for a temp job with the decorating crew. And I only applied two days ago."

"Maybe someone had been watching you, following you," Jackson suggested.

"That's possible. Maybe the woman who took my son has been keeping an eye on me. Maybe she wants to make sure I can't ID her."

"Can you?"

She made a slight sound of frustration and closed her eyes a moment. "I wish. But the only thing I can remember is that it was a woman. She warned me to be quiet or the gunmen would kill me. She also said they might take the baby to get me to cooperate."

Jackson tried not to let that get to him, but it had to have been terrifying. "Maybe this woman is the one who hired the intruder. She could have sent him here, not for me or Caden, but for you. She could have done that to cover up the fact that she stole your child. Maybe she wants you dead."

Not a sound of frustration this time, but her eyes widened with surprise. No. Make that shock. "But why kill *me?* I don't know who she is."

"She might not realize that. If she believes you could identify her, then she would want to keep you on the run, away from the police. And if she thought she could no longer do that, then she might hire someone to kill you."

"Oh, God." And Bailey kept repeating it. With each repeat, she grew paler and her breath started to race. "I can't believe I didn't make the connection. I thought the intruder was here after you or even Caden—maybe a kidnapping for ransom. How could I have been so stupid?"

Jackson was about to point out that the intruder could indeed have been there for a kidnapping attempt. Of course, that still left the question of why the man had implicated Bailey?

"I've considered the possibility that the intruder somehow eavesdropped on my conversation with Evan," Jackson explained. "When I talked to Evan in the foyer, I said your name and asked him to run a background check on you. If the intruder heard that, using some kind of long-range eavesdropping device, he might have latched on to it because he would have known I was already suspicious of you."

She frantically shook her head. "Or he already knew my name before he arrived."

That was his number-one theory. "But if this woman who stole your baby wants you dead, why try to have you killed here at the estate? Why not wait until after you left? There's a long stretch of country road between here and San Antonio, and if the intruder had attacked there, fewer witnesses would have been around."

Bailey shuddered. "I don't know why it happened the way it did. But I can't pretend that man didn't come here looking for me. That means I brought the danger here with me. I'm sorry for that. I was so desperate to find out the truth about Caden that I failed to remember it might not be safe for me to come here."

Jackson couldn't argue with any of that. Except he, too, had been threatened by those mysterious letters. Now, the question was, were the threats connected? He couldn't immediately see how, but then he didn't like the timing of the latest letter and Bailey's arrival at his estate.

"I'm sorry," she repeated. She turned quickly and headed for the door.

Jackson hurried after her. "Wait. Where are you going?" He caught up with her just outside his office and stepped in front of her.

"Far away from here. I'll call you about the test results." She swallowed hard. "I swear, I didn't mean to put Caden or you in danger."

"The danger was here before you arrived," he conceded. Part of him wanted to step aside and let her leave, but he wasn't stupid. This particular Pandora's Box had already been opened, and whether Bailey left or not, he didn't think the danger would go with her.

When she tried to dart around him, Jackson put her against the wall again. Hell. He'd been manhandling Bailey a lot lately, but he wasn't going to let her leave until she saw the whole picture.

Even if it was a picture he wasn't sure he wanted her to see.

"This is a theory," he started, "with a lot of *if*'s. But it's a theory that kept me up most of the night. If this mystery woman did indeed hire the intruder to kill you, and if she also arranged Caden's adoption, then she might want to cover that up as well. That might be the reason she sent the hired gun here to the estate."

Bailey uttered another, "Oh, God."

Yeah. Oh, God *summed it up.*

She grabbed on to handfuls of his shirt. "You have to beef up security—"

"I already have. And my house manager is in the process of getting even more guards out here. Trust me, Caden will be safe."

The breath swooshed out of her, and she dropped her head onto his shoulder. Even though he couldn't see her face, he had no doubt that she was crying. Jackson could feel her knotted muscles, and he heard the sob she was trying to hold back in her throat. He hadn't needed anything else to convince him that Bailey was on the up-and-up, that she truly was just trying to find her missing baby, but her reaction was definitely more proof that she was the victim here.

She lifted her head, met his gaze. "Why aren't you throwing me out?"

Jackson was asking himself the same thing. He was

good at coming up with the angles, and one angle was that he should keep her close, just in case that payoff would become necessary. But his usual heart of stone didn't feel so stone-cold all of a sudden.

He wanted to help her. Even if that meant facing a truth he didn't want to face.

Jackson cursed, and that caused her forehead to bunch up. No doubt she was wondering what he was cursing about. But this profanity was for *her*—for those needs she stirred deep inside him.

She stood there, her breath hitting against his mouth. Her incredible blue eyes wide with concern.

And with her body pressed against his.

Jackson especially noticed that body-to-body part.

He was responsible for it. After all, it had been his manhandling that had resulted in her being against the wall again.

There was a moment, just a split second, when his body started to think below the belt again. A moment where he wondered what it be like to kiss her.

How did she taste?

And were those lips as soft as they looked?

Jackson felt himself moving in closer. His body revved up, everything inside him preparing for something that damn sure shouldn't happen.

He breathed in her scent, some kind of floral shampoo maybe. But beneath the bottled stuff was something that was all woman. Something warm and silky. Something that triggered his asinine male brain into thinking that kissing her was a good idea after all.

Her eyelids fluttered down. A velvety feminine sound left her mouth. Her body moved slightly closer, brushing against his.

Everything about her was soft. Her skin. Her scent. Even that clingy cotton dress that was now pressed against his jeans and shirt.

"This shouldn't happen," she whispered.

Even though her voice was soft as well, it was the hard mental slap that Jackson needed. He jerked back and tried to rein in that stupid urge to haul her to him and kiss her until neither one of them had any breath left.

"Sorry," he mumbled.

He was ready to fumble with an explanation about the danger creating the heat between them, but thankfully the house phone on his desk rang. He felt thankful for a moment before he remembered this was the line his staff would use if there were any other problems with security.

Jackson hurried into his office to grab the phone.

"It's me," Steven Perez said. With just those two words, Jackson could hear the concern in his house manager's voice.

"A problem?" Jackson asked.

"Could be. Ryan Cassaine is at the front gate."

The adoption attorney. "Why is he here?"

"He won't say. He claims it's important, but I checked your calendar, and you don't have any appointments."

No. But he did want to see Ryan so he could clarify that everything had been aboveboard with the adoption. "Let him in," Jackson instructed.

"He's not alone," Steven interjected. "He has a woman with him. Shannon Wright."

Jackson thought he might have misheard. "Shannon Wright?"

"Yes, sir. She's one of the two women you asked me to investigate."

He had indeed. Jackson had asked Evan and the sheriff to do the same. After all, Shannon Wright was a suspect in the disappearance of Bailey's son. The hired gun had also used his cell to call her. "What does she want? And better yet, why is she here with my adoption attorney?"

"Neither one of them is volunteering much to me, but Shannon is insisting that she talk to you. She says she has to tell you something important about your son."

Chapter Six

Everything seemed to be happening so fast that Bailey had trouble catching her breath. In the past twenty-four hours, she'd encountered an armed intruder, saw the precious child that might be her own and had flirted with danger by nearly kissing Jackson.

And now a suspect she'd been trying to question for four months had shown up on Jackson's doorstep.

What the heck was going on?

That was something she didn't get a chance to ask Jackson, because the moment he gave his house manager permission to escort Shannon Wright and Ryan Cassaine onto the estate, Jackson began a flurry of calls.

Some of those calls involved background requests on Shannon, but most were about security and moving Caden to the panic room. However, he also phoned Evan, his business manager, to see if he knew anything about this visit. Judging from what she could hear, Evan didn't have a clue, but he was on his way back out to the estate as well.

Maybe with the DNA results.

As critical as those results were, however, Bailey had to put the thought of them aside so she could focus on this meeting. Was it possible Shannon had come to confess that she had indeed taken Caden? If so, that could be as critical as the DNA results.

"Come with me," Jackson told Bailey when he ended the call. "I don't want this meeting to take place in the house while Caden is here."

Bailey agreed. She had no idea what the attorney's role in any of this was, but Shannon was a suspect in a newborn's kidnapping. Plus, the intruder had called Shannon. Her number was on his cell phone, and Bailey wanted an explanation for that, along with the rest.

"Shannon could be armed," Bailey pointed out as she followed Jackson down the stairs.

"Steven, the estate manager, will search them both."

Good. But Bailey wouldn't breathe easier until Shannon said what she had apparently come to say and then was off the estate and far away from Caden. Or arrested. If the woman confessed to kidnapping the baby, then Bailey would make sure Shannon was hauled off to jail.

Jackson led Bailey through the house and to the sunroom. It faced an elaborate garden that still had spots of green despite the winter weather.

Bailey looked out the glass at the approaching car and the three people who exited when it came to a stop. She recognized Steven immediately, but it took her a moment to realize the stocky woman in the billowy gray dress was indeed Shannon Wright. In the picture Bailey had, and the last time she'd spotted her, the woman had been a brunette, but now Shannon was sporting auburn hair that was cut short and choppy.

The tall, dark-haired man walking next to Shannon

was no doubt the adoption attorney. He spared Bailey a glance.

Shannon didn't spare anything. When she caught sight of Bailey, her mouth dropped open, and she came to a dead stop. Either Bailey's presence was a genuine surprise, or Shannon was faking it so she would appear innocent of having any dealings with the intruder.

"Strange bedfellows," Jackson mumbled. He glanced at her. "You okay?"

"Yes," Bailey lied.

Jackson must have known that, because he gave her arm a gentle squeeze. It seemed so…intimate. But Bailey accepted it as a gesture of comfort. Too bad Jackson was the last person from whom she should be seeking anything except information, but she kept finding herself drawn to him.

Steven ushered the visitors inside the sunroom, but he didn't come in. He stayed on the other side of the glass as if standing guard. Good. Because Bailey had no idea what could happen during this so-called meeting. It could simply be an attempt to set her up for another attack.

"Ryan," Jackson greeted. He shook hands with the attorney. "This is Bailey Hodges."

Everything about the man seemed uncomfortable. His shoulders were pulled back. His facial muscles, tight. His mud-brown eyes were narrowed and filled with suspicion.

"First thing this morning, I got a call from Evan, several calls in fact," Ryan said, without bothering to introduce Shannon. "He said you have some questions about the adoption. Not a good time for this, Jackson, considering the adoption will be final two days after

Christmas. If you had questions, you should have called me directly when we started this process."

"I didn't have questions *then*." In contrast, Jackson kept his voice calm. He looked laid-back and casual in his jeans and white shirt with rolled up sleeves. However, Bailey sensed the storm brewing beneath the cool facade. "Obviously, I have them now. Questions for you, too," he said, turning that lethal gaze on Shannon.

With that, Jackson sat on the wicker sofa and waited. Because Bailey's legs weren't feeling very steady, she sat as well. Eventually, so did Shannon. Ryan continued to stand and hover over them.

"I know who you are," Shannon volunteered, staring at Bailey. "You followed me. Hounded me," she amended. "And all for no reason. I didn't take your baby."

Bailey listened to each word, replaying them in her head. Even though she had wanted to meet and talk with Shannon for months, this was Bailey's first chance to hear the woman speak. Shannon had obviously been avoiding her, just as Bailey had been avoiding the cops.

Was this the same woman's voice she'd heard in the hospital?

"I'm innocent," Shannon persisted. "Though I'm guessing you don't believe that, because I got a call that SAPD was looking for me again."

Bailey wasn't sure she bought the woman's denial, and judging from the rumbling sound that Jackson made deep within his chest, he was skeptical as well.

"You could have told us this with a phone call," Jackson pointed out. "Instead you opted for a face-to-face meeting, with my adoption attorney no less. How do you two know each other?"

"She called me out of the blue last night," Ryan jumped to explain.

"I'd read he was your attorney," Shannon continued when Ryan didn't add anything else, "and when I realized that SAPD still considered me a suspect, I called Ryan." She huffed and looked at Bailey. "SAPD has questioned me more than a dozen times. The same questions over and over again. And I still have the same answers. I didn't take your baby. I didn't even see you during the hostage standoff. The first chance I could, I got out of there and haven't been back since."

Bailey lifted her shoulder. "Then if you're innocent, why call Ryan?"

"Because I learned from a cop friend that SAPD was questioning Ryan, too. At first I thought that was good, that I was no longer a suspect. But then I realized they were trying to connect *me* to Ryan and some moron who tried to break into your estate yesterday."

"An armed moron," Jackson supplied. "Who had called you just hours before he came here."

"So the police said." Shannon moved to the edge of her seat so she was closer and eye-to-eye with Bailey. "I don't know the man who came here. I never spoke to him, and I have no idea why he called me."

Bailey was about to suggest a reason—because Shannon might be neck-deep in all of this—but Jackson spoke before she could say anything.

"You didn't know the gunman, and you didn't know my adoption attorney. Am I supposed to believe that? After all, you're here together."

Shannon mumbled something under her breath, then

said, "I'd never met or spoken to Ryan Cassaine before last night. I said I needed to clear up some things with you and asked him to drive me out here. I wasn't sure you'd let me in if I came alone."

"I wouldn't have," Jackson assured her.

Shannon snapped back her shoulders and stared at him.

"Shannon didn't give me a stolen child," Ryan explained, sounding more frustrated with each word. "No one did. And everything about that adoption was perfectly legal." He paused, then shook his head. "Jackson, I can't believe you'd think I would do something like that. You asked me to find a baby. A private adoption. And that's exactly what I did."

Bailey didn't blindly accept that. "You don't think there's any chance, even a slight one, that Jackson's adopted son is my missing baby?"

"No." But Ryan had no sooner said that when he dodged her gaze.

Mercy, was the man hiding something?

"You were with Caden's so-called birth mother when she delivered him?" Bailey pressed Ryan.

"Of course not. Jackson asked me to find a baby, so I did some checking. I put out a lot of feelers, and soon I got the call from the birth mother. And she's not 'so-called.' She is his birth mother."

"Go over the details of that again," Jackson insisted.

Ryan huffed, louder this time. "She called me hours after she gave birth and told me that she wanted to give up her baby for adoption. A healthy baby boy. But she had no insurance and a lot of medical and credit card bills. She also wanted to go back to college. So, as you know, I contacted you, and together we came up with a sum to compensate her."

"How much compensation?" Bailey wanted to know. And she looked at Jackson for the answer.

He shrugged. "A million to the birth mother, and then there were Ryan's legal fees."

A million dollars. That was probably a drop in the bucket for Jackson, but Bailey figured there were many people who would have sold a baby for that amount or less.

Her baby.

She turned to Ryan. "What proof do you have that this woman actually gave birth to Caden?"

"The usual documents. Hospital records. The application for a birth certificate. A statement from the midwife who assisted with the delivery."

"They could have been faked." Bailey slid her gaze to Shannon. "And someone who works in a hospital would have known how to fake them."

That brought Shannon to her feet for another round of denial. Ryan got in on it as well.

"Quiet!" Jackson ordered. It wasn't a shout. It didn't have to be. Jackson had a way of commanding attention. "I want to talk to the birth mother."

Ryan was shaking his head before Jackson even finished. "Impossible. Evan has already tried and failed. She demanded a closed adoption, and you agreed. That was all part of the deal."

"Renegotiate the deal," Jackson insisted. "Offer her more *compensation*. All I want is a simple conversation."

Ryan glared at Bailey as if she were the cause of this demand. And she was. But Jackson seemed to be on a quest for the truth as well. Was that because he believed Caden wasn't her son and therefore she wasn't a threat to the adoption?

"I'll make some calls," Ryan finally conceded. "I'll see what I can do."

Jackson didn't thank the man, but instead looked at Shannon. "And as for you, I'd like you to take a lie-detector test."

Shannon looked at him as if he'd lost his mind. "SAPD gave me one and I passed."

"Then you shouldn't mind taking another. I have a friend who teaches at the FBI Academy in Quantico. He's a truth analyst, and he uses some cutting-edge technology that's several steps beyond the normal lie detector."

Bailey examined Shannon's expression. The woman seemed even more uncomfortable than she had when she first arrived, but then maybe anyone would be in her position. Bailey so wanted it to be Shannon who had taken the child, because Shannon was here, right in front of them, and if she confessed, then it could all be over. She would know what had happened when the mystery woman walked out of the hospital with her newborn son.

But Shannon didn't appear to be on the verge of confessing anything.

"All right," Shannon told Jackson. "Schedule the lie-detector test and I'll take it."

Bailey was both surprised and relieved, though agreeing to the test was one thing. Taking it was something else.

"Will you help me clear my name?" Shannon said,

and it took Bailey a moment to realize that the woman was talking to her and not Jackson.

"I'm doing everything to find my son," Bailey told her. "And if finding him helps clear your name, then of course I'll help. But if you're guilty, if you are the one who took him, I want you to tell me now."

"I didn't take him." Tears sprang to the woman's eyes. "I swear I didn't."

Ryan couldn't have looked more disinterested about Shannon's emotional response. He checked his watch and glanced impatiently at his car. "I need to get back to my office and contact the birth mother."

"Or you could give me her number and I'll contact her myself," Jackson offered.

"I don't have her number, only her attorney's. Since it's the holidays, it might take me a while to reach her. She's likely on break from her college classes."

"You'll find her," Jackson said with complete certainty, and in such a way that it sounded like a threat.

Ryan didn't miss the undertone. The attorney's jaw tightened again, and he motioned for Shannon to follow him.

"I'm innocent," Shannon insisted one more time before she left with Ryan.

Jackson and Bailey stood there and watched them drive away. Steven followed behind them in his truck, probably to make sure they left the grounds.

"Well?" Jackson asked. "Did you believe everything they said?"

"I'm not sure. You?"

"I never believe anyone until I have proof."

"You believed me," she reminded him.

That brought his gaze to hers. And he nodded. "I

believe your son is missing. I believe someone wants to harm you. I believe you're searching for the truth."

"And if I find the truth?" she asked cautiously.

"The truth doesn't change, even if it's hard to accept." He stared at her. "I've had Caden for nearly four months now, since he was a week old."

She knew what he was saying. She hadn't even held her son, but Jackson had been Caden's father. And even though she might indeed be the little boy's mother, she was a stranger to him.

Yes, the truth was often hard to accept.

And in this case it was heartbreaking.

Jackson turned, eased his arm around her and pulled her to him. This didn't feel like a veiled threat. It didn't feel intimidating.

Unfortunately, it felt right.

It would be so easy just to take what he was offering her. But Bailey pulled back.

"Does this chemistry between us have something to do with Caden?" she asked.

Those dangerous gray eyes narrowed slightly. "Do you mean am I pretending to be attracted to you? No," he answered before she could respond.

He pulled her to him again. "Trust me, if I could feel differently about you, I would. You're a threat, plain and simple, and yes, I have been thinking about how to neutralize the threat." He stayed quiet a moment. "But then I've also been thinking about kissing you."

That both frightened and excited her, because she'd been thinking about kissing him, too. "I'm not faking the attraction either," she confessed. "That means we have a problem."

Jackson was so close now, practically right in her

face, looking down at her. The corner of his mouth lifted, causing a dimple to flash in his cheek. A dimple. On any other man, that might have added a touch of wholesomeness to dark, rugged looks, but his looks were nowhere in the realm of being wholesome.

In a fantasy, Jackson would have been the pirate. A Wild West outlaw. Or the vampire who had his deadly desire barely under control. A face and body perfect for seducing and drawing women in.

But she suspected he'd never had to seduce a woman in his life.

"Are you as bad as I think you are?" she asked.

Mercy. There was too much breath in her voice, and she sounded as if she were under his spell. Heck, she was. Maybe that vampire fantasy wasn't so far off the mark.

He nodded. "Once, I was attracted to a business rival, and I slept with her. The next week I did a hostile take-over of her company."

For some stupid reason, that made Bailey smile. What was wrong with her? She should be pulling away, but the sound of his voice and that half smile made her feel all warm and golden.

"I'm not a nice guy," he added. And he lowered his head and touched his mouth to hers.

Bailey felt as if she were melting.

She'd expected his mouth to be slightly rough and warm. It was. She'd expected him to know how to kiss.

He did.

But even with all those expectations in place, she was still shocked at what he was doing to her. It was as if he knew just the right pressure, just the right angle to draw as much from the kiss as was humanly possible. This was the reason people kissed and fantasized about kissing, she decided. So they could feel this slow hunger slide right through them.

The moment was perfect: the sun-washed room, the devil in the great-fitting jeans who had her in his arms, her body yielding to the pressure and heat that his mouth had created.

Bailey lifted her hand to slip it around the back of his neck and draw him closer, but she stopped at the last second. What she didn't do was stop the kiss. She couldn't. She began to tingle, the sensation starting at her mouth and gliding through the rest of her. Everything inside her suddenly wanted this.

And more.

It had been so long since she'd had *more,* and she'd never had the likes of Jackson Malone. Kissing him was playing with fire, and that still didn't make her pull away.

Jackson was the one who stopped. He blinked and stared down into her eyes. "That was better than I thought it would be," he complained. "And my expectation had been pretty high."

Yes. She knew exactly what he meant.

Thankfully, Bailey didn't have to voice that, because his cell rang. And just like that, the moment was lost. Good thing, too. One kiss shouldn't feel like hours of foreplay. It shouldn't leave her body with a dull ache that only one thing would cure. And that one thing was someone she couldn't have or kiss again.

Jackson answered the call, but continued to study her. "Evan," he greeted, after glancing at the screen.

That was it. All he said. But it snapped her back to

reality and out of the land of kissing foreplay and wild fantasies. A good thing, too, because this call could be critical. Again, Bailey couldn't hear the conversation, but she prayed Evan had the DNA test results and that the results would prove that Caden was hers.

Jackson didn't exactly put on a poker face. As he listened, his jaw muscles went to war with each other. His mouth bent into a snarl.

"Find out what happened and get someone down to that lab immediately. If there's been any kind of breach in privacy, I want to know about it."

That finished sobering her up. *Sweet heaven. This certainly didn't seem like good news.*

"What happened?" she asked, the moment he hung up.

"The lab misplaced the DNA test results."

"What?" Her mind began to race. Had the woman who'd stolen her baby somehow got the results so that Jackson and she couldn't learn the truth?

"Don't go there yet," Jackson mumbled. "It's the holidays. The lab is working with just a skeleton crew, so the tests could still be there, but maybe misfiled."

She shook her head. He seemed so calm about this. Maybe too calm. "But someone might have tampered with them."

"Evan's taking a second set to another lab."

And that brought her to yet another concern.

"Can I trust Evan?" she asked. "Would he doctor the results to get me out of the way?"

"No," Jackson said with complete confidence. "He might insist that I lie to you. He might even try to handle getting you out of the picture on his own. But he would tell me the truth."

Hopefully, Jackson would do the same for her, but Bailey had to be realistic. She needed to figure out how to get her own sample of Caden's DNA so she could compare it to the stored umbilical cord.

"Don't borrow trouble," Jackson murmured. He put his hand on the small of her back to get her moving inside.

But Bailey didn't move a single step when she heard the loud noise.

A blast of some kind.

Everything happened fast. Too fast for her to figure out what was going on. One second she was standing, and the next moment she was on the floor of the sunroom where Jackson had pushed her.

She looked back at Jackson, ready to ask what was going on, but the next sound clarified things for her.

Something slammed into one of the sunroom panels and sent glass spraying over them.

My God.

Someone was shooting at them.

Chapter Seven

Jackson pulled Bailey to the side of the sofa.

It wasn't a second too soon.

Another bullet came tearing through the sunroom, shattering the glass and sending the dangerous spray of jagged pieces right at them.

"Caden!" Bailey shouted, covering her head.

"He's in the panic room." Jackson was beyond thankful for that. The panic room was bulletproof and impossible for anyone to penetrate, unless they knew the security codes. His son was safe.

Jackson couldn't say the same for Bailey and him. Their lives were on the line.

Whoever the hell was doing this would pay and pay hard. Of course, the question was, who was firing those shots? And with all his safeguards in place, how the devil had anyone gotten onto the grounds?

"Not again," Bailey mumbled. "Please God, this can't be happening again."

She couldn't keep from remembering the hostage situation at the maternity hospital and reliving the nightmares that came with that fateful day. Jackson couldn't stop the flashbacks, not for her or himself. Images of the bodies from the plane crash came back at him like lethal bullets. But he wouldn't let that old trauma im-mobilize him and stop him from figuring a way out of this life-and-death situation.

"Stay down," he warned Bailey, and he pushed her all the way to the floor.

Jackson tried to shelter her as best he could, but it was next to impossible. They were literally in a glass room, and the delicate wicker furniture didn't provide much protection. Added to that, he didn't have any weapons he could use to defend them.

More shots came, each of them eating through what was left of the glass and tearing into the furniture. Jackson made sure Bailey stayed flat on the floor so it would minimize the shooter's kill zone, but he figured this measure wouldn't save them for long.

He had to get Bailey out of there.

But how?

Jackson glanced back at the entry into the main house. The door was wide open, but it was a good twenty feet away. They could crawl to reach it, but that was twenty feet wide out in the open. A lot of bullets could come at them during that short space.

In between the din of the bullet barrage, Jackson could hear the shouts from inside the house. No doubt his staff was trying to figure out what to do. Someone had already called 9-1-1. Steven had almost certainly been alerted. Help was on the way.

But help might come too late.

The next round of bullets came directly at the sofa. And that told Jackson a lot about the shooter. He was probably using a rifle with a high-powered scope. In other words, the gunman knew exactly where Bailey and he were. It also told him something else.

The shooter might not even be on the estate.

It was possible their attacker was positioned in one of the tall trees that grew along the estate walls. As long as the walls themselves weren't touched, it wouldn't have triggered the security system and therefore wouldn't have alerted anyone on his staff. Of course, Jackson had considered something like that would be possible, but since he'd spent his entire life without being shot at, he had never considered it to be a real threat.

But it was real now.

"What do we do?" Bailey asked.

She was shaking, but her voice was surprisingly strong and determined. Good. Because she would need every ounce of strength and determination to get out of this alive.

"We have to move," Jackson told her, knowing that this might not be the right thing to do.

Hell, it was possible they didn't have any right moves. But he couldn't blindly accept that they were going to die today. Somehow, he had to figure out a way to stay alive for the sake of his son. He intended to raise his little boy, to love him, and Jackson wouldn't let some SOB take away Caden's father.

He glanced back at the entry that seemed to be getting farther away, and he spotted José, one of the gardeners. The terrified-looking man was holding a rifle, and he lifted it, no doubt questioning Jackson about what he should do.

Jackson wanted him to return fire, hoping it would give him an opportunity to get Bailey into the house.

"Can you get the rifle to me?" Jackson shouted.

The young man gave a shaky nod, and he got down

into a crouching position so he could inch toward the entry.

More bullets slammed into the sofa. But not just there. A spray of shots went into the entryway where José was making his way toward them.

"Stop!" Jackson told José. "The shooter must be able to see you."

Probably through a long-range scope on his rifle. And that meant, if the gunman could see José, he wouldn't have any trouble homing in on Jackson and Bailey if they tried to dive through the entryway.

But what choice did he have?

They couldn't just lie there and wait.

"Where's Steven?" Jackson called out.

"On his way," José relayed. "He was at the gate."

No doubt ushering out their guests. Hopefully, Steven was armed and was already trying to pinpoint the shooter so he could try to take him out. Or at least create a diversion. And that gave Jackson an idea.

He could create his own diversion.

"Everyone inside, get down," he instructed. Jackson had to yell over the sounds of the gunfire. "José, crawl toward the window and lift the rifle so it can be seen. Stay down though. Don't get anywhere near the window."

Because, if the shooter took the bait, it wouldn't be long before the bullets went that way.

"Get ready to move," Jackson told Bailey, and he got her into a crouching position so she could scramble to the entryway, a move that would happen only if the diversion worked.

The seconds crawled by, and with each one, Jackson had to fight to stay calm. Timing and a clear head were everything right now, and he had to focus solely on getting Bailey out of there.

"I'm lifting the rifle now," José called out.

Jackson could no longer see the young man, or for that matter, the window where he had positioned himself. But he had immediate proof that José was there.

The shooter shifted his aim, and the bullets blasted through the window.

"Stay down!" Jackson reminded everyone. But as he was shouting out that order, he grabbed onto Bailey's arm.

They had one chance at this. Just one. Because once they were out in the open, the shooter would no doubt turn those bullets back on them.

"Now!" Jackson shouted, making sure that Bailey heard him.

He turned, placing himself behind her and began to shove her toward the entry.

Bailey didn't have time to think. She scrambled forward, with Jackson pushing her toward what she prayed would be safety. Somehow, they had to get out of this nightmare.

In the back of her mind, she realized that Jackson was protecting her. He had taken the most dangerous position, placing himself behind her like a human shield. Bailey didn't want him to take that kind of risk, but it was too late to reverse things. The only thing that counted now was speed, because the sooner they got inside, the safer they would both be.

She hoped.

Bailey prayed this wasn't some full-scale attack. If so, Caden could be in danger.

Each step seemed to take a lifetime. Probably because

she had no breath and her entire body was a tangle of nerves and adrenaline. They were just a few feet away when the bullets shifted again. Away from the window, and back to Jackson and her.

Several shots slammed into the jamb around the entryway and tore through the wood. Still, Jackson didn't stop. He made a feral sound of outrage and rammed into her, shoving her through the entry.

Bailey landed hard on the floor, knocking what little breath she had right out of her, but she still managed to latch onto Jackson and haul him inside with her.

Jackson looped his arms around her and rolled to the side, away from the gaping entry. Some of the bullets ricocheted off the marble floor and careened into the walls and furnishings.

"Everybody get out!" Jackson shouted, and his staff began to scramble.

Jackson dragged her behind a large stone coffee table and pulled her back to the floor.

"José, I need that rifle. And I need you to take Bailey to the panic room. When you get there, give Tracy the code word, 'silver rose,' and she'll let you in." Then he turned to Bailey.

Somehow, she managed to shake her head. Bailey wasn't objecting to the panic room order. She wanted to go there. She wanted to be as far away from those bullets as possible. But she wanted Jackson, José and anyone else in the house to go with her.

"What are you going to do?" she asked Jackson.

Every muscle in his body was rock-hard and primed for a fight. His face was misted with sweat despite the cold air gushing in through the broken glass.

"I'm going after this SOB," Jackson insisted.

"No!" But she might as well have been talking to herself because Jackson motioned for José to switch places with him.

They did, and the moment José had hold of her arm, Jackson signaled for them to get moving.

"No!" Bailey repeated. "Think of Caden. He needs you."

"I *am* thinking of Caden." Jackson took the rifle and checked to make sure it was loaded. "José, get her out of here."

Bailey wanted to argue. She wanted to convince Jackson not to do this, but another round of bullets sent José and her running for their lives. The shooter might not be able to see them inside the house, but with the bullets bouncing off all the marble and stone, it wasn't safe to be anywhere near a window or exterior door.

Of course, that meant Jackson was right in the line of fire.

José had a death grip on her arm and sprinted with her toward the center of the house. She could still hear the gunfire. Heavy, thick blasts. Each of them potentially lethal. And she prayed Jackson would have backup soon.

"This way," José told her, and he led her into a library that was on the same floor as the sunroom.

There were floor-to-ceiling shelves lined perfectly with books, but there was also a floor-to-ceiling window on the far center wall. José didn't take her anywhere near that. He pressed a button beneath one of the shelves, and a small book-size monitor dropped down. Bailey immediately saw the nanny, Tracy Collier. She looked as terrified as Bailey was.

"Mr. Malone says I'm to tell you 'silver rose,'" José said to the woman.

Tracy nodded and turned from the screen while she pressed in some numbers on a keypad behind her. A moment later, the shelf slid back to reveal a metal door. Bailey heard the locks disengage, and José opened it. Tracy was there, just on the other side, and the nanny was armed.

"Stay here," José insisted. "I'm going to see if I can help Mr. Malone."

Good. She wanted Jackson to have all the help he could get, but she had second and third thoughts about going into hiding while Jackson and José were taking all the risks.

"Mr. Malone's orders," José reminded her, and he pushed her inside and shut the door.

Bailey was ready to pound on the door, but then she looked around the room. Tracy and she weren't alone. Two of the housekeepers were there as well, and they were standing against the far wall, apparently waiting for the nightmare to end.

The room wasn't that large compared to the rest of the house. Probably twenty by thirty feet. There was a sofa, several chairs, a fridge, desk and a storage cabinet.

And then she saw Caden.

He was sleeping on a thick quilt stretched out on the carpeted floor.

Oh, mercy.

Again, she was hit with all the feelings of motherhood. All the things she had missed in the past four months. Bailey didn't know if this baby was hers, but she felt the love pour through her heart.

"The sheriff just arrived," Tracy whispered.

Bailey tore her gaze from the baby to look at the monitor set into the wall. Actually, it was a series of monitors, six of them in all, and they showed various parts of the estate.

"There," Tracy said, pointing to the monitor that displayed the front gate. The sheriff's vehicle was indeed there, along with two other cars, and they were making their way to the estate.

"What about Jackson?" Bailey asked. She frantically searched the screens but didn't see him. She didn't see the shooter either, and since the panic room was apparently soundproof, she couldn't hear if there were shots still being fired.

It seemed to take forever, but Bailey finally spotted him. Jackson was out of the now-shredded sunroom and was in the rose garden. He had the rifle and had taken cover behind a marble statue.

"He shouldn't be out there," Bailey mumbled, and she put her fingers to her mouth to stop her lips from trembling.

Here, she barely knew Jackson, but he had risked his life for her. He had saved her from those bullets. And now he was outside, continuing to risk his life so he could make sure Caden would stay safe.

She glanced at Caden again and understood his need to protect that precious little baby. The gunman, whoever he was, had to be stopped. Killed, even. Bailey didn't want a repeat attack.

Volleying glances between the baby and the monitors, Bailey watched as Jackson leaned out from the statue. He took aim.

And fired.

The recoil snapped his shoulder back, but he quickly

re-aimed and fired again before taking cover. For a moment she thought he was going to repeat the process all over again, but he stopped and looked in the opposite direction.

Where the sheriff was approaching.

Two deputies got out of their vehicles and fanned out over the garden. She saw Steven, the estate manager. He was armed, and he followed behind one of the deputies. Along with the sheriff, they all began to walk toward the west fence, partly concealed by clusters of trees and shrubs.

The sheriff said something to Jackson and then motioned toward the estate. It was clear from Jackson's expression that he was arguing, but he soon turned and began to race back into the house.

Bailey's heart dropped.

My God. What was happening now? Had the gunman managed to get into the house?

"No one can break in here," Tracy reminded her. "There's another panic room where most of the household staff went, and even they can't get into this one without the password and then me punching in the code to the locks."

That made Bailey breathe a little easier, but Jackson was still out there, possibly under the same roof with a would-be killer.

Tracy adjusted one of the monitors, switching to a camera inside the house. Jackson was running through the foyer and toward the library.

Behind them, Caden made a sound, and Bailey saw his eyes open. It wasn't a happy sound, either. He immediately started to cry.

"Pick him up," Tracy said to no one in particular. She

hurried to the door, probably to wait for Jackson so she could let him in.

Bailey glanced at the two housekeepers. They were still huddled in the corner with their arms wrapped around each other. One of them moved, as if to go to the baby, but Bailey got there first.

Her heart was pounding out of her chest by the time she leaned down and picked up Caden from the quilt. He didn't stop crying, and it actually got worse when he looked at her. No surprise there. She was a stranger to him, and he had just woken up in a strange room. He was scared.

"Shhh," Bailey whispered. She brought him closer to her, snuggling him against her chest, and she started to rock, hoping it would soothe him.

It worked.

The sobs turned to a whimper, and he stared at her as if trying to figure out who she was. Bailey was sure she was staring at him the same way. He felt like hers, but she couldn't dismiss that serious emotions were playing into this.

Tracy punched in the codes, and the door slid open. It was Jackson of course. His gaze fired all around the room until his attention landed on her.

Part of her was so relieved to see him, to know that he was safe, but he put the rifle aside and immediately went to take Caden from her arms.

Bailey thought her heart might have literally broken at that moment.

Jackson didn't ask why she was holding his baby, and he didn't have to voice his disapproval. She saw it there, all over his face.

"Where's the gunman?" she managed to ask.

Jackson kissed the top of Caden's head and hugged him, maybe a little too tightly, because Caden protested.

"I don't know," Jackson answered. He kept a firm hold on Caden while he checked the monitors.

Bailey checked them, too, and saw the sheriff and the others converge near the west fence. She held her breath, waiting and praying.

Jackson's phone rang, and Tracy put aside her weapon so he could hand her the baby. Bailey didn't have time to be hurt that he hadn't offered Caden to her. That's because she was on pins and needles waiting for an update.

But Jackson didn't say anything. He just listened to the caller.

"Where?" Jackson asked. But it was more like a bark than a question.

Sweet heaven, whatever he was hearing, it obviously wasn't good news.

"No," Jackson said a moment later. "I'll make the arrangements."

Jackson ended the call, snared her gaze and then took a deep breath. "The gunman wasn't on the estate," he told her. "He launched the attack from one of the trees just behind the fence. The sheriff just found what appears to be his vehicle, dozens of spent cartridges…and some other things."

Bailey took a step closer, almost afraid to hear the answer to the question she had to ask. "And the gunman?"

Jackson shook his head. "He got away on foot. But the deputies are in pursuit."

Oh, God. Jackson didn't have to spell out what that meant. There could be another attack. Maybe soon.

"What should we do?" But Bailey was already considering the possibilities. This danger was linked to her. She was the one the gunman was after.

"I should leave," she said before Jackson could speak. "If I go, the gunman won't come back to the estate."

Jackson went to her and slipped his arm around her waist. "You're wrong. Yes, it appears the gunman was trying to kill us. But a rifle wasn't the only thing he had with him. In the vehicle, he had an infant seat and baby supplies."

She shook her head, not understanding. "Why?"

"Because he didn't just come here to kill us, Bailey. He came here to kidnap Caden."

Chapter Eight

Jackson sank down in the chair behind his desk and drained the shot of whiskey he'd just poured. He swore to himself.

It was the first time he'd had a few minutes to himself since the attack in the sunroom, and even though he was well aware of how close Bailey and he had come to dying, the alone time allowed everything to sink in.

He cursed again.

Someone wanted him dead. And worse, that someone wanted his son.

Who the hell was doing this? And better yet, why? If he knew the *why,* he would probably know the *who*.

He glanced at the threatening letter again: "Jackson Malone, I won't forgive and forget. Watch your back."

It was pretty generic for a threat. There were plenty of people he'd crossed while taking his company to the billion-dollar level. But why would someone he'd trampled over in the business world want to go after Caden?

They wouldn't, he decided.

A person out for that kind of revenge would go after the company. Since the company was no longer Jackson's top priority, it would be easier to try to worm into the investments and create some havoc. But there had been no such attempts on Malone Investments.

So that brought him back to Bailey. Now, this is where the pieces fit.

Someone, a woman, had taken Bailey's newborn, and maybe this woman was afraid of being caught. Of course, that theory worked only if Caden was indeed Bailey's missing son.

Or if someone believed he was.

Jackson glanced at his laptop, which showed split screens of the estate and grounds. There were people and law enforcement officers milling around both inside and out, most either working on the investigation or putting the new security measures in place. Jackson had hired new guards—as many as he could get on such short notice—and a new security system was being installed.

On another monitor, he saw Bailey in the nursery with Tracy and Caden, who was taking his afternoon nap. Tracy was reading a paperback, but Bailey was sitting, staring at Caden.

Keeping watch.

While Jackson didn't care much for the idea of Bailey spending time bonding with Caden, he welcomed the extra set of eyes and ears. Especially Bailey's. If someone tried to get to Caden, she would die protecting the baby. He had no doubt about that, and right now he wanted to do any- and everything to protect his little boy.

That included learning the truth.

Jackson took out his phone and called Evan.

"Are you okay?" Evan asked, the moment he answered.

"No," Jackson answered honestly. He was dealing with the adrenaline crash from hell, and he still wasn't completely confident of his security measures.

"I've been looking into places where you could take Caden," Evan went on. "How about your ski lodge in Colorado? It's at the top of the mountain, and it might be easier to control security."

Jackson had already considered it. He'd also considered his other properties. Or maybe his parents' villa in France.

"The problem is, that no matter where I go I have to set up security." And not just any ordinary security. It had to be all-encompassing. "At least here at the estate, I already have people and equipment in place."

"Yes, but is it a good idea to stay here?" Evan pressed.

"It will be, if we can get to the bottom of what's happening." Jackson looked at the security screens again and saw Bailey leaving the nursery. He watched as she stepped into the hall and headed toward his office. No doubt she wanted an update, and Jackson hoped he was about to get one.

"What about the DNA test?" he asked Evan.

"The lab found the samples and they're running them now. We might have results by the end of the day."

Well, that was…progress at least.

"I do have some information on the background checks I ran on the two women from the maternity hospital. Shannon Wright and Robin Russo. I just emailed you an interesting financial report on Shannon. And as for Robin, well, she's actually in the waiting room right outside my office."

That grabbed Jackson's attention. "Why?" He

continued to watch Bailey. She was looking around, as if she expected someone to jump out and attack her.

"Robin wants to see Bailey and you. Apparently, the renewed interest from SAPD has unnerved her, and she wants to try to convince you that she's innocent."

"Is she?"

There was a soft knock at his door, and Jackson got up to let Bailey in. She was leaning so close to the door that she practically spilled into his arms. Jackson put his hand on her waist, to steady her.

And to touch her, too.

She seemed to need some kind of reassurance, and Jackson suddenly felt more than willing to give it to her.

"I'm not sure if Robin is innocent or not," Evan answered. "Do you want to talk to her and ask her yourself?"

Jackson caught Bailey's gaze. "You think it's a good idea if we have a meeting with Robin Russo?"

Bailey's eyes widened and she nodded. "Yes, especially if Robin can give us any information about who launched this attack."

Jackson wasn't sure they would get that from the woman, but since the danger could very well be linked to what happened at the maternity hospital four months ago, he didn't think it would hurt to hear what Robin had to say.

"Bring her out to the estate. To the guesthouse," Jackson corrected.

"But isn't the guesthouse where Bailey is staying?" Evan questioned.

Not any more. But since Bailey didn't know that yet, Jackson kept it to himself. "Just bring Robin and get me those DNA test results," Jackson insisted, and he ended the call.

"Robin is coming here?" Bailey asked.

"Yes. Evan is leaving his office with her now, but I won't bring her inside the house itself." Of course, last time that hadn't worked very well, since their attacker hadn't even gotten on the grounds, and yet he'd managed to do some serious damage to both to the estate and Bailey's and his peace of mind.

Bailey scrubbed her hands down the sides of her dress. "Well, at least the sheriff and his deputies are here in case something goes wrong."

True. The timing was in their favor anyway. "I'll have her searched for any weapons before she'll be allowed through the gate," he explained. Though again, would that be enough?

"Tracy said you're installing a new perimeter security system," Bailey commented.

Man, her nerves were right there at the surface. Her mind was probably still firing on all cylinders as well, but he was betting the adrenaline crash had left her beyond exhausted. It certainly had for him.

"I am. There are sensors that will detect anyone or anything that gets near the fence. I'm having the fence reinforced as well."

More hand rubbing. "Must have been hard to get all the workers here, with Christmas just two days away."

It was. But money spoke loud and clear, even if the workers would rather be spending this time with their families.

"Evan said he emailed me some updates on Shannon Wright and Robin Russo," Jackson told her, hoping it would get her mind off all the security details he was already obsessing over.

One obsession at a time, he reminded himself.

But then he made the mistake of looking at Bailey.

There it was. That punch below the belt. She looked so feminine and soft, the exact opposite of how she made him feel. And those eyes… Her eyes always seemed to be giving him some kind of invitation unintentionally.

Still, she was attracted to him, too. He could feel that as well.

But feeling it and acting on it were two different things. He couldn't control his body's response to her, but he sure as hell could control what he did about that response.

Jackson hoped.

Mentally groaning, he opened the email Evan had sent him and read through the reports. Bailey moved behind him, her hand gripping the back of his chair. Her fingers brushed against his shoulder.

So much for hoping. She might as well have kissed him.

He was toast.

"Both women seem to have some financial issues," Bailey said, obviously reading the email and hopefully not noticing his reaction to her touch.

"Yeah," Jackson agreed, forcing himself to concentrate on the reports. This was damn serious stuff, and he shouldn't be thinking about her softness, her eyes, or any other part of her.

"Evan thinks Shannon is living beyond her means," she concluded. Bailey moved closer, dipping down so that her head was right next to his. "She certainly has a lot of debt for her income."

She did. About fifty thousand dollars in credit card bills and loans. But that made her appear to be a poor money manager, not necessarily a baby snatcher.

"If she'd sold your son, then Shannon would have gotten a chunk of that one million dollars. So why hasn't she used the money to pay off her bills?"

"Maybe she knew if she used the cash right away, it would draw attention to her," Bailey pointed out. "After all, the police are still investigating her."

True. And that meant Shannon could have the money stashed offshore somewhere. Or maybe she had used it to a pay for a hired gun or two.

Bailey's warm breath hit his neck, and she slid her hand around the outside of his arm so she could touch the screen.

Great.

Now, he could feel her and take in her scent, too. Added to that, she was close enough to kiss. He couldn't think about kissing her, because that last session nearly had him dragging her off to bed. Not the way to keep the distance between them.

But maybe there was no need for distance.

Maybe he could take her and still be objective about this investigation.

He rolled his eyes. *Sheez.* An aroused man could come up with all kinds of stupid justifications for kissing an attractive woman.

"Look at this." Bailey tapped the report on Robin Russo. "Robin Russo recently bought a house and paid cash."

Now that was a massive red flag, and he wondered if SAPD knew about it. Of course, there were a lot of reasons why someone might pay cash, but paired with

Robin's presence at the hospital the day of the hostage crisis, it made the transaction suspicious.

"I'll have Evan dig deeper into her financials," Jackson added. "And we can ask her about it when she's here."

Bailey pulled back slightly, but still stayed close. "Why do you think she wants to see us?"

"Probably to get us to back off any investigation. Even if she's innocent, it can't be fun to have the cops examining her every move."

At least he hoped that's what the cops were doing. He also hoped SAPD still had both Shannon and Robin under surveillance, because if either of the women had hired the gunmen, there might have been some kind of contact or face-to-face meeting to make the payment.

"What are you thinking?" Bailey asked, still staring at the screen.

He could have given her a good answer. Nothing sexual. Nothing to do with kissing. One that proved to her that he was pouring over every detail of Evan's report. But he had already absorbed the details. He was good at that—taking huge chunks of information and processing them quickly.

Still, there were things to be done.

Jackson would have to contact SAPD about that surveillance question. He would need more financial info on both women. He wanted to check for offshore accounts. And he'd do all those things and more. But for now, he had to get something off his chest.

Or rather *on* it.

Hell. He was going with his gut here, and not his business brain, because he was reasonably sure his brain would get outvoted by the rest of him.

Bailey was still so close to him that he didn't have to move far. Jackson simply reached out, slid his hand around the back of her neck and eased her down to him. He took his time. Kept the motion slow and easy so she would have a chance to back away.

But she didn't.

Bailey moved closer as well, and their mouths met.

Her lips were soft. There was that word again. *Soft.* But he couldn't remember soft ever feeling so damn good. However, it was more than just pleasurable. Jackson felt that jolt deep inside him. Familiar but different. This felt like something more than just a reaction to a really good kiss.

It couldn't be more.

Kissing Bailey was a bad enough complication, but making more out of it than it really was could be a huge mistake. They weren't friends. Or lovers. Even though it suddenly felt as if they were.

"Oh," she muttered, stretching out the syllable so that it sounded dreamy. "You're a really good kisser."

That was information he didn't need to hear. Though it made him smile.

Toast.

Yes, that's exactly what he was.

"You're not so bad yourself," he let her know.

"Really? Because I think this is all your doing. I think I'm under your spell."

Good. Because he didn't care why she was melting into him, only that she was. He wanted Bailey hot, wanting and ready. And she was getting there fast.

She made a feminine sound when the tip of his tongue touched hers. That sound created another jolt of heat and need. The jolt got stronger when she slipped her arm around him, turning her body so that she was directly in front of him.

Finally, she was against his chest.

He could feel her breasts. Small but firm. He dropped his hand from the back of her neck to her waist, and he pulled her onto his lap.

Jackson figured he'd lost his mind. But he no longer cared. The only thing that he could think of right now was taking Bailey.

FREE Merchandise is 'in the Cards' for you!

Dear Reader,

We're giving away
FREE MERCHANDISE!

Seriously, we'd like to reward you for reading this novel by giving you **FREE MERCHANDISE** worth over **$20**. And no purchase is necessary!

You see the Jack of Hearts sticker above? Paste that sticker in the box on the Free Merchandise Voucher inside. Return the Voucher promptly...and we'll send you valuable Free Merchandise!

Thanks again for reading one of our novels—and enjoy your Free Merchandise with our compliments!

Pam Powers

Pam Powers

P.S. Look inside to see what Free Merchandise is **"in the cards"** for you!

(H-I-12/10)

W

e'd like to send you two free books to introduce you to the Harlequin Intrigue® series. These books are worth over $10, but they are yours to keep absolutely FREE! We'll even send you 2 wonderful surprise gifts. You can't lose!

REMEMBER: Your Free Merchandise, consisting of **2 Free Books** and **2 Free Gifts**, is worth over $20.00! No purchase is necessary, so please send for your Free Merchandise today.

YOUR FREE MERCHANDISE INCLUDES…

2 FREE Harlequin Intrigue® Books

AND 2 FREE Mystery Gifts

FREE MERCHANDISE VOUCHER

2 FREE
BOOKS
and
2 FREE
GIFTS

Please send my Free Merchandise, consisting of
2 Free Books and **2 Free Mystery Gifts**.
I understand that I am under no obligation to buy
anything, as explained on the back of this card.

*About how many NEW paperback fiction books
have you purchased in the past 3 months?*

❏ 0-2   ❏ 3-6   ❏ 7 or more
E9TM   **E9TX**   **E9UA**

❏ I prefer the regular-print edition   ❏ I prefer the larger-print edition
182/382 HDL   **199/399 HDL**

Please Print

FIRST NAME

LAST NAME

ADDRESS

APT.#   CITY

STATE/PROV.   ZIP/POSTAL CODE

NO PURCHASE NECESSARY!

► Detach card and mail today. No stamp needed. ►

© 2010 HARLEQUIN ENTERPRISES LIMITED. ® and ™ are trademarks owned and used by the trademark owner and/or its licensee. Printed in the U.S.A.

(H-I-12/10)

BUSINESS REPLY MAIL
FIRST-CLASS MAIL   PERMIT NO. 717   BUFFALO, NY

POSTAGE WILL BE PAID BY ADDRESSEE

THE READER SERVICE
PO BOX 1867
BUFFALO NY 14240-9952

NO POSTAGE
NECESSARY
IF MAILED
IN THE
UNITED STATES

▲ If offer card is missing write to: The Reader Service, P.O. Box 1867, Buffalo, NY 14240-1867 or visit www.ReaderService.com ▼

Chapter Nine

Bailey couldn't breathe. She couldn't stop her heart from racing. And she definitely couldn't stop herself from touching Jackson.

But what she could do was feel.

Oh, yes. She could do that all right.

She was suddenly aware of every inch of her body. And Jackson's. That probably had something to do with the fact she was now on his lap. Her hands were on his chest and on all those toned muscles that she had fantasized about. Now she didn't have to fantasize. He was hers for the touching.

So she touched.

Bailey slid her hand down to this stomach and had the pleasure of feeling those muscles respond. Jackson responded, too. There was a deep rumble in his throat, and he snapped her even closer.

The kiss deepened and got even hotter. She couldn't remember the last time she'd been swept away like this. And all with just kisses. If he could set these kind of white-hot fires inside her with just his mouth, it left her breathless to think of what it would be like to make love with him. He wouldn't be gentle. Not Jackson. She was betting he was as take-charge and thorough in bed as he was in business.

And Bailey was burning to find out if that was true.

She felt his hand on her leg. On her bare skin. And while he kept up the intensity of the kiss, he slid his palm up, pushing up her dress along with it.

In the back of her mind, she realized this was too much too soon. She hardly knew him. They had a ton of other things they should be doing. But in the front of her mind, Bailey could only feel the electric sensations he was creating.

His hand stopped midway up her thigh.

She wanted him to move higher. She wanted him to take this to the next level, even if that meant having sex on his desk. The thought of that shocked her.

And made her even hotter.

She'd never had sex on a desk. Never had sex with a man like Jackson. But she was betting it would be an experience she'd never forget.

He brought everything to a standstill, pulling back just slightly so they could make eye contact.

"You aren't going to stop me, are you?" he asked.

Bailey felt herself blush, but she wasn't actually embarrassed. The fire was too hot for that, and she was still trying to figure out if she wanted to keep pressing. It wouldn't take much. After all, she was on his lap and she could feel the proof of his arousal.

He was ready to do what she was fantasizing about.

Well, physically ready anyway.

She saw the doubt in his eyes, doubt that mirrored in hers.

"I was just…" But she didn't know how to finish the

statement. *I was just going to let you do whatever you wanted to me? I was just too hot to stop?*

No.

Best not to pour out her raunchy thoughts like that. Besides, Jackson already knew that she wanted him. It wouldn't help this situation to spell it out.

"Should I apologize?" he asked.

Bailey got up from his lap, not easily, and smoothed down her dress. "Don't you dare."

Jackson smiled, causing that killer dimple to wink in his right cheek. But the smile quickly faded. "So what should I do?"

His words dripped with carnal undertones. "Not that," she murmured, giving him a quick kiss. "You were right to stop."

"Really? Because it doesn't feel right."

Oh, the man was a charmer, and coupled with those incredible hot looks, he was charming her right into his bed—or his desktop.

The phone on his desk buzzed, but it was several long moments before Jackson tore his gaze from hers to answer it.

Sweet heaven.

What was she going to do about this untimely attraction?

"Let them in," she heard Jackson say, and then he hung up the phone. "Evan is on his way with Robin Russo."

That required Bailey to take a deep breath.

"You don't want to see her?" Jackson questioned, obviously not missing her reaction.

"No. I do. I've met her before. Actually, she's the one who filed the restraining order against me because I was following her. I thought she might have answers about my missing son."

"She never volunteered anything or let anything slip?"

Bailey shook her head. "But then I wasn't very subtle. I was desperate. Still am." She paused. "Which is probably why you should handle the questions. When I see Robin Russo and Shannon Wright, my instincts are to shake them senseless until they tell me what I want to hear—that one of them took my son, that he's safe and that he'll be returned to me immediately."

Jackson slid his hand over hers. "Maybe that'll happen today."

She didn't miss the slight catch in his voice, perhaps because if that miracle did happen, it could mean they would learn that her missing son was Caden. And that would create even more of a firestorm than this insane attraction between Jackson and her.

He patted her hand and stood. "I've changed my mind about meeting them in the guesthouse," he let her know. "I don't want you outside just yet. So I'll have them brought into the sitting area just off the foyer. Fewer windows in there."

And not too far from the front door. Bailey approved of that, even though she doubted they were going to have to toss Robin or Evan out of the house.

Jackson typed in some keys on his laptop and tapped into the video feed from the nursery. She saw Tracy in the rocking chair next to the crib. Caden was still sleeping. Maybe he would continue napping through this meeting, and then Bailey could sneak back up to the nursery. Jackson hadn't exactly issued an invitation for her to visit with Caden, but he hadn't objected to her presence there after the shooting.

He touched the screen, running his fingers along Caden's sleeping face. Then he huffed and opened his desk drawer. He took out a small handgun and slipped it into the back waist of his pants.

"It's just a precaution," he assured her, probably because she didn't completely choke off a gasp.

Good. Despite the surprised gasp, Bailey wanted to take all possible precautions. She didn't want another attack like the last one.

While they walked toward the stairs, Jackson made a call. "Tracy," he said. "It's time to move Caden into the panic room."

Yet another precaution Bailey approved of, even though it would probably wake him. The baby had already had too much of his routine disrupted, and that riled her. This needed to end so that Caden could have some normalcy.

Jackson led her down the stairs and into the foyer. They walked past the tree and Bailey made a mental note to finish decorating it if the danger—and—life settled down long enough for that to happen. It seemed a little trivial in the grand scheme of things, but she wanted Caden to have as much of a Christmas experience as possible.

Even if she wouldn't be there to share it.

Bailey had to accept that, despite the hot kisses they'd just experienced, Jackson could at any moment demand that she leave.

They'd just made it into the sitting room when the front door opened, and Steven ushered both Evan and Robin inside. Robin gave her a cool glance, followed by a huff. Evan's reaction was more of an eye roll. He obviously didn't want Bailey there at the estate, encroaching on his boss's territory.

Robin had a different reason for that huff.

It had been only a month since Bailey had last seen Robin. Or rather, since she'd last watched the woman. Bailey had sat in her car across from the medical clinic where Robin now worked, and waited for her to come out. Bailey had followed her, praying that Robin would lead her to any clues about the baby. But nothing came of it. Robin had merely done some grocery shopping and had then returned to her apartment. Hardly incriminating.

Like now.

Robin was the picture of propriety, with her sleek shoulder-length brunette hair, perfectly styled. Her makeup was perfect as well. And she looked holiday festive in her emerald-green business suit that was almost an exact match with her eyes. Which were narrowed.

"You wanted to speak to us," Jackson prompted.

"To *you*," Robin clarified, turning her entire body in Jackson's direction. "I haven't had much luck convincing Miss Hodges that I didn't take her son."

Jackson shrugged and sat on the sofa with Bailey. "Why do you think that is? Have you done something to make Bailey suspicious?"

That didn't improve Robin's narrowed eyes. "I was at the wrong place at the wrong time. The San Antonio Maternity Hospital should have provided better security. They didn't. And because they didn't, those gunmen were allowed to storm in and take the hostages. I was nearly taken myself, but I managed to duck into a supply closet."

"Lucky you," Jackson commented, taking the sarcasm right out of Bailey's mouth.

Bailey had also been at the wrong place at the wrong time, and she'd had her child stolen. Possibly by this woman.

God, she wished she could remember the face and the voice of the person who'd walked out of that room with her child. Ironically, this person had saved Bailey, but Bailey would have traded her own life to know that her son was safe.

"I understand Shannon was already here," Robin said a moment later.

Both Jackson and Bailey looked at Evan who confirmed that with a nod. "I told her. She also knows there was a gunman. She wanted to come anyway."

"To tell you to back off," Robin said to Bailey. She sank down onto the love seat across from Bailey and Jackson. "I don't have time for more investigations. I'm trying to get on with my life. So should you."

"Not without my son," Bailey fired right back. "And not until I find him and the person responsible for taking him."

"Robin insists she had no part in that," Evan volunteered, causing all three of them to turn in his direction.

"I can speak for myself," Robin snapped. "But he's right. I didn't take your son." Instead of a huff, she gave a heavy sigh, and her expression softened. "I'm sorry for your loss, Bailey. I truly am. But I can't go through another round of this investigation."

"You sound stressed," Jackson commented. "Does that have something to do with moving? I understand you recently bought a house."

Robin blinked and gave an accusing glare at Evan. "I suppose you're the one who told him that."

Evan paused but finally nodded. "Jackson and I would like to know where you got the money."

"None of your business," she barked and got to her feet. Robin pointed her perfectly manicured index finger at Evan. "You said this would be a fair meeting. No ambush. You said they would listen to what I had to say."

"We listened," Jackson assured her. "But I'm not so sure we believe you. I'm certainly not going to ask SAPD to call off the investigation."

Robin gave an indignant nod. "Then don't expect me to cooperate. I'm leaving here and going to the police. I'll file charges against Bailey for harassment."

Bailey started to get up and tell the woman to take a hike, but Jackson caught on to her arm and kept her anchored to the sofa.

"I don't think you want to take on Bailey," Jackson warned Robin. "Because if you do, you'll be taking on me. You think you can handle that?"

Her chin stayed high, but Robin dropped back a step. "No. But I won't be bullied. Don't think I won't play dirty, too. I'll announce to anyone who'll listen that Bailey is hiding out here with you." She turned that venomous gaze on Bailey. "It's my guess you don't want certain people to know where you are."

Mercy. Robin must have known about the attempts on Bailey's life, because that had been all over the news, but did the woman also know that Bailey had been followed? And that the two gunmen who'd come to the estate could be linked to her as well?

Robin didn't wait for Bailey or Jackson to respond.

She stormed out of the room and toward the front door. Jackson sprang from the sofa and hurried to watch her. Probably to make sure she did indeed leave.

"My advice?" Evan said. He went to Jackson's side but waited until Robin had closed the door behind her before he continued. "Don't put any more heat on Shannon Wright or Robin Russo. Just let me quietly handle this."

"Quietly?" Bailey wanted to scream. "My son is missing, and I don't want to stay quiet. Besides, you're the one who brought her here."

"Only because I thought it would smooth things over."

"Nothing will be smoothed over until I find my son." Bailey had to fight hard to hang on to her temper. She was sick and tired of being stonewalled and placated. She only wanted her baby back.

"Antagonizing Robin won't help," Evan tossed at her.

"Maybe not. But those DNA results will. Where are they, by the way?" She glanced at Jackson to see what his reaction was to her grilling his business manager, but he only looked at Evan, apparently waiting for him to answer her question.

"I'm working on it," Evan snapped. He aimed a why-aren't-you-defending-me glare at Jackson.

Jackson only shrugged. "I want those results, too."

Evan mumbled something and headed out, keeping the same rapid pace that Robin had when she made her exit. He slammed the front door behind him.

"Sorry about that." Jackson quickly went to the front door, locked it and reengaged the security system, using a keypad on the wall. Then he went to the window and watched Robin and Evan drive away.

"What are you thinking?" Bailey asked, unable to read his expression.

"I'm thinking I need to do some digging on Evan."

"I agree." She was glad they were on the same page. She also wanted the DNA tests repeated. "Do you think Evan might hold a grudge against you for his fiancée's death?"

"Maybe." He didn't say anything else for several moments. "Before today, I looked for any signs of that. Any subtle clues that Evan blamed me for that crash. No clues, subtle or otherwise. But then, Evan's a smart man. It's the reason I hired him to help manage my company."

Bailey thought about that a moment. "It doesn't make sense though. That plane crash was six months ago. If Evan had wanted revenge, he would have taken it then."

"Maybe. And maybe he's upset now because I'm truly happy for the first time in my life. Caden's adoption is just a few days away from being finalized. Plus, I've been thinking about selling my company."

"What?" This was the first she'd heard of that, and it certainly hadn't been mentioned in the papers.

Jackson lifted his shoulder. "I want to adopt another child, and I don't want to put in long hours at work. If I sell Malone Investments I can start a small consulting business. Evan suspects what I'm about to do, and I'm pretty sure he doesn't approve."

No, he wouldn't, because it would essentially mean he was out of a job.

Jackson checked his watch then looked at her. "I'm

moving both Caden and you into my suite. For security reasons," he quickly added.

Her heart gave a little leap. His suite? "You're sure? I figured you'd want me gone, not underfoot."

"Part of me does want you gone," he admitted. Then he shook his head. "But I can't send you away with someone trying to kill you."

Her heart leaped for a different reason. "Maybe that's exactly the reason I should go. As long as I'm here—"

He pressed his fingers to her mouth. "The last gunman came to kidnap Caden. This is no longer just about you. We're all in the middle of it."

True. But she was surprised Jackson had been able to accept that. She certainly hadn't come to terms with it yet.

He checked his watch again and took out his phone. "I'll call Tracy and tell her it's okay to come out of the panic room. Why don't you go on up and check on Caden for me?"

Bailey was thrilled to do that, but she didn't budge. "Why? Is anything wrong?"

"No." Jackson's answer was fast and sharp. "Just go on up and meet them as they come out of the panic room. I won't be long."

Bailey studied him a moment longer and finally nodded. There was no way she would give up a chance to spend some time with Caden, even if she suspected that Jackson might be up to something.

She went up the steps, glancing back at Jackson. He glanced at her, too, and motioned for her to go. She did. But because she couldn't shake the feeling that something just wasn't right, she stopped in the hall.

And waited.

She watched as Jackson did indeed make a call. From her position, she could even hear the beeps as he pressed in the numbers.

"It's Jackson Malone," he said to whomever answered. "Do you have those DNA test results for me?"

Bailey shook her head. She didn't think he was talking to Evan, so what was this about? Why would he be calling anyone but Evan about DNA results?

"I see," Jackson said a moment later. His back was to her, but she watched as he pressed his fingers to his forehead. "No. I'm still here," he continued.

Bailey inched even closer because she didn't want to miss any part of this. What was Jackson doing?

"Repeat the tests," Jackson said to the caller. "When you get back the second test results, call me. Then destroy the samples. I don't want anyone else to know what you just told me."

Chapter Ten

Jackson eased off the sofa in his suite and tiptoed to the crib so he could check on Caden. His son was still asleep, thank God, because he'd had a restless night. Probably because of the change of rooms. But Jackson had had no choice. He'd wanted both Caden and Bailey nearby, in case there was another attack.

It was the reason Jackson had kept not one gun but two by his side throughout the night. That was a first for him. He'd never woken up to guns on Christmas Eve day.

He leaned down and brushed a kiss on top of Caden's head. The baby stirred a little but didn't open his eyes.

"My son," Jackson mumbled.

That was certainly how he felt about the baby; but soon, very soon, he was going to have to come to terms with the fact that Bailey felt the same way about the little boy. Jackson had been wrong to think he could offer her money. Wrong to think he could intimidate her into leaving. Besides, he didn't want to intimidate her. And that was a problem in itself.

He wanted her in other ways.

Thankfully, they hadn't had time to act on those

"other ways." Jackson had been tied up with security arrangements and calls about updates in the investigation. All of that had lasted well into the night, and by the time he'd returned to his suite, both Bailey and Caden were asleep. He'd considered waking Bailey because there was something important he had to tell her.

He had to tell her about the call he'd made after Robin and Evan left.

That call had been critical. Life-changing, even. But when Jackson gave her the news, he wanted her to be alert so they could talk it out. He decided that talk could wait until morning.

Well, it was morning now, and even though he was dreading what he had to tell Bailey, he couldn't put it off much longer. The day was likely to get hectic fast. Hopefully, that wouldn't include any new dangers. They had enough of those as it was.

Jackson gave Caden another kiss and made his way to the adjoining bedroom. His bedroom, normally. But this morning Bailey was sleeping in his bed. She was co-cooned there in the center of the massive bed, snuggled beneath the white, goose down comforter.

Completely covered except for her bare leg.

And her thigh.

All that bare skin revved up his body. Not that he needed much to rev him. All through the night, his body kept reminding him that Bailey was close enough to touch. Close enough to kiss. And even close enough for him to get off the sofa in the sitting room and climb into the bed with her. Then they could continue what they'd started the day before in his office.

Jackson was still staring at her thigh when he heard a slight sound. His gaze slid up higher, and he saw that Bailey was not only awake, she was staring at him with sleepy eyes. She was obviously aware that he was gawking at her.

She smiled. It was sleepy and slow as well. She clearly wasn't fully awake.

"I dreamed about you," she whispered. And from the sound of it, it had been a hot dream.

"Oh, yeah?" Jackson came closer and sank down on the bed next to her. "Because I dreamed about you, too."

He leaned over, working his fingers into her hair, which was fanned against the stark white pillow. In fact, Bailey was the only spot of color amid all that white. And she looked better than any dream he'd ever had.

So Jackson kissed her.

She made a wistful sound of pleasure, rolled toward him and slipped her arm around him. Bailey might have still been half asleep, but she did a darn good job of kissing him right back. And more. She drew him closer—and closer—until she pulled him on top of her. Since his shirt was unbuttoned, his bare chest landed against her flimsy gown and her breasts.

Jackson glanced back into the sitting room. He couldn't see Caden's crib from this angle, but the suite door was locked and secured with the new security system, and he figured he would hear Caden if he awoke.

Bailey lifted her leg, sliding it around his, pulling him even closer to her. Jackson responded all right. He got rock hard, and he deepened the kiss. Yeah, it was probably a stupid idea to do this, but Jackson figured there was no way he was going to talk his body, or hers, out of a quick round of morning sex.

But then she stopped.

Bailey just froze.

Jackson pulled back and stared down at her, trying to figure out what was wrong. For one thing, she no longer looked sleepy or aroused. Her eyes were wide, alert and somewhat accusing.

He pulled back farther. "What's wrong?" Because he didn't think he had misinterpreted the sexual signals she'd been sending him. Not just now either, but those signals and the attraction that had been there from the moment they met.

She sat up and adjusted the comforter so that it was completely covering her body. "We need to talk."

A talk that would no doubt include the reminder that they were in danger.

"I heard you on the phone last night," she said, the tone of her voice as accusing as the look in her eyes.

Jackson shook his head. "When? I was on the phone at lot—"

"The call you made in the foyer."

Oh. That one. The call. The one that could change their lives forever.

"'I don't want anyone else to know what you just told me,'" Bailey said, repeating him verbatim. "What are you keeping from me?"

But Jackson didn't get a chance to answer. The phone next to his bed buzzed. He considered ignoring it so he could finish this conversation, but it might be important. Plus, the sound apparently alerted Caden, because he started to cry.

"We'll finish this talk later," Bailey insisted, and she got up from the bed so she could pick up Caden.

Jackson cursed under his breath and took the call.

"It's Ryan Cassaine. I'm here at the estate."

"Really?" Jackson didn't bother trying to sound civil. "At this time of morning?"

"It's important, and it couldn't wait. I have Shannon Wright with me, and we need to see you immediately."

"Shannon?" Jackson didn't sound civil about that, either.

"The last time you two were here, Bailey and I were attacked. And Shannon is one of our suspects."

"She wouldn't have orchestrated that attack," Ryan countered without hesitation. "Just let us in and listen to what Shannon has to say. I can promise you, when she's done you'll be convinced that she has no desire to harm Caden or you."

Jackson still wanted to say no, but he couldn't. Did Shannon have some kind of proof that she hadn't offered during her last visit? It certainly sounded like it.

"I'll meet you in the downstairs sitting room in ten minutes," Jackson told Ryan. And he hoped like hell this was worth the worry that it would no doubt put Bailey through.

"You're meeting them again?" she asked, the moment he hung up. Yes, there was the worry in her voice. She probably hadn't forgotten the talk they needed to have, but the possibility of renewed danger overshadowed it.

Jackson nodded, then phoned Steven so he could let the pair in. "Search them both," Jackson reminded Steven.

Then he went to Bailey. She had a fussy Caden in her arms and was rocking him.

"I just need to hear what Shannon has to say," Jackson

insisted, and he left it at that. He headed to his closet so he could get ready.

"I'm going with you," Bailey said from the other room. He heard her use the phone to call for the nanny.

Jackson wished he could do this alone, just in case this was some kind of ruse to launch another round of gunfire. But he also figured he stood zero chance of talking Bailey into staying put. So that meant he needed to find out what Shannon had to say so he could end this meeting as soon as possible.

When he came out of his dressing room, Bailey wasn't there. Tracy now had Caden in her arms.

"He's hungry," Tracy let Jackson know. "I'll be in the nursery with him."

"Keep your phone close," Jackson warned her, and he placed his gun in the back of his jeans. "I might have to move the two of you and Bailey back to the panic room."

Tracy's eyes widened. "Not more trouble?"

Jackson wanted to assure her that wasn't the case, but lately, trouble seemed to have an easy way of finding him.

They went into the hall, but Jackson didn't head for the stairs until he made sure that Tracy and Caden were indeed in the nursery. And then he waited for Bailey. He didn't have to wait long. Within seconds she came out of the room next to his where her clothes and toiletries were now stashed. She'd changed and was now wearing another loaner dress. This one was a dark green.

"You could stay with Caden and Tracy," Jackson reminded her.

But as expected, Bailey just shook her head and

headed down the stairs. Yes, she was as anxious for the truth as he was, but she was also no doubt equally anxious for that private conversation the two of them needed to finish.

By the time they made it to the bottom of the stairs, Steven had opened the front door, disengaged the security system and was ushering in their guests.

"This better be worth our time," Jackson warned both Shannon and Ryan.

"It is," Shannon assured him, but she didn't say anything else until they were all in the room just off the foyer. Even then, it took several moments for her to continue. "You might want to sit down for this."

Bailey and Jackson exchanged glances, and Jackson decided it was a good time to show both Ryan and Shannon that he was armed. He did sit, but he took out his gun and placed it on the table next to him. Bailey sat next to him, so that either of them would be able to reach the weapon if necessary.

Shannon already looked ready to jump out of her skin, but this upped her anxiety significantly. Jackson could see sweat popping out above her upper lip, and she had a death grip on her purse.

"I lied to you," Shannon finally said, aiming that remark at Jackson. "Well, at least I lied by omission. What I didn't tell you…" She took a deep breath and blinked back tears. "What I didn't tell you was that I'm Caden's birth mother."

The room went deadly silent.

Jackson's gaze flew to Bailey, and she'd gone ash pale. She was holding her breath and staring in disbelief at the woman who'd just dropped a bombshell.

"You're Caden's mother?" Bailey challenged.

Shannon started to sob now, and Ryan sat beside her and put his arm around her.

"I didn't know until this morning," Ryan explained.

"This doesn't make sense." Bailey shook her head. "You were working in the hospital the day that Caden was born. There's no way you could have given birth on that day, and there was no mention in the investigation of your being pregnant."

"Because I hid the pregnancy." She plucked at her oversized caftan dress. "People just thought I was gaining weight, and I didn't tell them any differently."

"Why would you do that?" Jackson pressed.

Shannon swiped at the tears that spilled down her cheeks. "My family is very conservative, and they would have disowned me for having a child out of wedlock. So I hid it from them, too."

The tears were genuine, but Jackson figured that was the only thing about this story that was. "And what about Bailey's question? Caden was born on the day of the hostage situation."

"The day after," Shannon corrected. "I gave birth to him in my apartment. Delivered him myself. I had arranged for a private adoption, but it fell through. So when I heard you were looking to adopt a child, I had a friend call Ryan Cassaine. I had the friend lie and say she was a college student who needed compensation for her medical bills and tuition."

"Oh, God," Jackson heard Bailey say, and he also heard the enormous pain in her voice.

Bailey clamped her teeth over her bottom lip, but it was too late. It was already trembling. So was she.

"He's not my son," Bailey mumbled. "Caden's not

mine." She got up from the chair and would have no doubt raced from the room, but Jackson caught onto her.

"I can't do this," Bailey insisted, and she broke free of his grip.

This time, when she tried to run Jackson didn't stop her. She hurried up the stairs. Jackson wanted nothing more than to go to her, but first he had to settle some business with Shannon.

"You have proof that you're Caden's mother?" Jackson asked.

She nodded and took an envelope from her purse. "That's a maternity test I had done right before I handed Caden over to Ryan. It proves he's my son."

Jackson took the envelope but didn't open it. "So what do you want? Why are you really here?"

"Not to claim my son. I want you to raise him, that's why I put him up for adoption."

"But you want more money," Jackson concluded.

Shannon dried her tears again. "I have debts, and if those were paid, then I could leave Texas. I could go live with my cousins in Seattle. I swear that you'd never hear from me again. The only thing I need other than the money, is for you to stop this investigation. If you press for the truth, my family will learn about Caden and they'll make my life a living hell."

Jackson's hands fisted, and he felt the envelope crush under the pressure.

"No," Jackson told her.

"No?" Shannon question. "No to what?"

"To the money and to stopping the investigation." Jackson didn't know who was more surprised by his refusal—Ryan or Shannon.

Ryan held up his hands in defense when Jackson aimed a glare at him. "I had no idea she was going to ask for payment. She came to me with the maternity test results and said she wanted to show you the proof, so that you'd have some peace of mind."

"I didn't want Bailey Hodges trying to scam you," Shannon piped in. She jumped to her feet. "I don't want much money," she concluded. "A hundred thousand is all, and that's chump change to a man like you."

"It's extortion," Ryan grumbled. "I'm sorry, Jackson. I really had no idea this is what she wanted to do." Ryan grabbed on to Shannon's arm and started to move her toward the door.

But Shannon dug in her heels and wouldn't budge. "A hundred thousand or whatever you happen to have in your safe right now. And for that, I go away. There'll never be any questions about me trying to regain custody of my son."

It took every ounce of his willpower not to throw her out the door. "Get her out of here," he told Ryan. "Now."

Shannon continued to resist, but Ryan shoved her out of the sitting room. "I'm sorry," he repeated to Jackson.

"You're the one who'll be sorry," Shannon insisted, looking back at Jackson. "A hundred thousand dollars is a small price to pay to keep my baby." And she repeated that threat all the way out the door.

"I'll make sure they leave the estate," Steven said, following them.

Jackson shut the door, rearmed the security system and glanced down at the envelope Shannon had given him. Hell. This was yet another issue that he would have to deal with. But first things first.

He had to check on Bailey.

Jackson retrieved his gun from the sitting room and headed up the stairs. He had no trouble finding her. All he had to do was follow the sound of her sobs. She was on his bed, her face buried in the pillows.

"I'm so sorry," she said without looking up at him. "I only wanted to find my baby. And by coming here, I've placed your son in danger."

Jackson drew in a long breath and went to her. He eased down on the bed and touched her shoulder, turning her so that he could see her face. Or rather, so she could see his.

"I'm the one who needs to apologize," he told her.

She stiffened slightly and swiped her hand over her eyes. Bailey studied his expression. "What do you mean?"

This wasn't a blow he could soften, so Jackson just decided to say what he had been keeping secret from her for the past twelve hours.

"Remember that call you overhead in the foyer?" he asked.

Bailey nodded. She pressed her hand to her chest as if to steady her heart.

"I had another DNA test done from the same samples I gave Evan. I wanted to verify the results with a second lab. Last night I got the results."

Her breath was uneven now, and she grabbed his shirt. "And?"

Jackson looked her straight in the eyes. "The DNA was a match. Caden is your son."

Chapter Eleven

"Wh-what?" Bailey managed to say. She scrambled to get to a sitting position, and she blinked back the rest of her tears so she could clearly see Jackson's face.

"According to the DNA, you're Caden's biological mother," Jackson repeated.

She heard the words, but it still took several seconds for them to sink in. She hadn't been wrong. Caden was her missing baby.

"Oh, God." Because she had no choice, she dropped her head onto Jackson's shoulder.

The relief flooded through her, and so did the other dozens of emotions. She'd searched so long, four months, and now she'd finally found her son. Not only was he alive, he was under the same roof, just a few rooms away.

But then her head swooshed off his shoulder. "Shannon lied."

Jackson nodded, and he tossed the envelope Shannon had given him onto the nightstand. "I figure her so-called maternity study is completely bogus. She is a nurse after all, so she probably used her medical training to fake a report that she thought would convince me to pony up some cash."

"But wouldn't Shannon have realized that you'd run your own tests to prove or disprove what she was claiming?" Bailey asked.

"Yeah, but maybe she thought I wouldn't be thinking too clearly after I saw that maternity study. She had her eyes set just on getting the money."

The relief and the joy were suddenly darkened by the anger that slammed through Bailey. "I want her arrested."

Jackson nodded again. "I'll deal with Shannon. And with Ryan, if he's had any part in this."

Of course. Ryan. A greedy adoption attorney could have helped set this up. It sickened and infuriated Bailey to think that either or both were willing to use her baby to extort money from Jackson.

He put his fingers beneath her chin, lifting it. "I owe you an apology. When I got that call last night, I intended to tell you, but I needed time to come to terms with what all of this meant."

His apology certainly seemed sincere enough, but Bailey remembered something else. "You told the person on the phone to destroy the samples and to keep the results a secret."

"I did," he readily admitted. "Because I didn't want anyone but us to know the truth. For now," Jackson added. "If the person who stole Caden from you realizes that you've found him, there might be other attempts to kill you. Other attempts to take him so this person can cover up his or her crime."

She couldn't argue with that. "But for hours you kept this to yourself."

"Yes." He paused, shook his head. "Like I said, I was

trying to come to terms with it. I wouldn't have kept it from you much longer."

Bailey believed him and wondered if she was a fool for doing so. After all, Jackson was a wealthy, powerful man, and he loved Caden. Just how far would he go to make sure he remained Caden's father?

The image of her precious little boy flashed into her mind. "I need to see him."

Bailey expected Jackson to try to stop her. She figured he would insist they talk before she went racing to her baby. But he didn't. Jackson got off the bed and stepped aside so that Bailey could race toward the suite door.

Her feet suddenly couldn't go fast enough, and she ran down the hall to the nursery. For several terrifying moments, she thought he might not be there, that Jackson had already sent Caden off somewhere so Bailey couldn't take him. But when she threw open the nursery door she saw that her son was in the nanny's arms. Tracy was seated in the rocking chair, an empty baby bottle next to her, and she was burping Caden.

Bailey obviously wasn't able to hide her raw emotions, and she moved much too quickly toward them. Tracy's eyes registered the alarm, and Caden turned his head, no doubt to see what the commotion was about.

Tracy looked past Bailey and to Jackson, and he simply nodded. That was it. His approval for Tracy to stand up and hand over Caden.

Of course, Bailey had held him before, but this time it was different. This time she wasn't holding Jackson's adopted son, she was holding her own baby.

She couldn't stop the tears and didn't even try. Bailey hugged Caden close and held on tight.

Finally. She had him, and she had no plans to let go.

"Give us some privacy, please," Jackson said to Tracy.

Tracy waited a moment, probably trying to figure out what was going on, but the woman finally gathered up the empty bottle and the bib and headed out the door.

Jackson didn't say anything else. He merely leaned against the wall and watched them.

Bailey didn't mind the audience. Heck, she didn't mind anything right now. She sank down into the rocking chair and sat Caden on her lap so she could see his precious little face.

He was perfect of course, and she went through the visual exam that most new mothers did of their newborns. She was four months late with this, but that didn't lessen her joy of counting ten little fingers and ten little toes.

Caden laughed when she wiggled his pinkie toe.

Bailey was certain that was the most miraculous sound she'd ever heard.

"He has my eyes," Bailey confirmed. There were pieces of her ex there, too, but they didn't bring back bad memories of a stormy relationship. On Caden, they were incredible features.

Caden reached for her hair, his chubby fingers pulling at the strands. Bailey laughed, too. These were the little miracles she had missed; but she would make up for all that lost time.

"D-d-d," Caden blurted out, and he looked at Jackson and gave him a big grin.

Jackson grinned back, but Bailey could see the pain in his eyes. It was a pain she understood all too well. She knew what it was like to lose a baby.

"Caden obviously loves you," Bailey mumbled.

"Yeah," Jackson said, but nothing else.

Bailey wasn't immune to what he was he feeling. Her own joy didn't make her blind or unfeeling to what Jackson was now experiencing. In fact, it only reminded her more that Jackson had risked his life for her son. He'd taken extreme measures and more to make sure Caden stayed safe. And in addition to that, Jackson loved Caden as much as her son loved him.

And that love caused Bailey's heart to sink a little.

What the heck was she going to do?

"Don't overthink it," Jackson warned, as if reading her mind. "For now, just get to know your son. We can talk later."

His generosity stunned her. Of course, she already knew he was an exceptional man, but that offer had no doubt cost him dearly. If their positions had been reversed, Bailey would have probably been doing everything within her power to hang on to Caden.

Jackson started to leave.

"Thank you," Bailey called out.

He turned back, gave her a slight smile and reached for the door. However, his phone rang before he could open it. He glanced down at the caller ID screen and groaned softly.

"It's the lab that Evan used to run Caden's DNA," Jackson let her know. He put the call on speakerphone and moved closer so she could hear. "Jackson Malone," he answered.

"Will Delaney. I'm the tech from Cyrogen Labs in San Antonio. Evan Young asked me to call you with the test results."

"And?" Jackson pressed when the tech didn't continue. Was it her imagination, or did the tech seem rattled?

"The two samples weren't a match," the tech informed them.

Bailey sucked in her breath. She couldn't believe what she'd just heard.

"The female's DNA that I tested couldn't possibly be related to the infant male," the tech continued. He hesitated again. "I hope these results are satisfactory?"

"Not really." Jackson tipped his eyes to the ceiling and mumbled something under his breath. "I'll get back to you. I need to call someone first."

Jackson slapped his phone shut and mumbled some harsh profanity, but he kept it at a whisper, probably because he didn't want Caden to hear his da-da curse a blue streak.

With Caden firmly in her arms, Bailey got to her feet. "You don't believe those results, do you?" And for one horrifying moment, she thought he might.

"No," Jackson assured her. "Evan no doubt told the lab to fake the results. If they ran the test at all. I'm sure he wanted to get the results he thought I wanted to hear." He met her gaze. "I wanted the truth, not a cover-up."

She released the breath she'd been holding. "Does Evan often do things like this?" Bailey thought of the threatening letter and Evan's strange behavior.

"Never." A moment later, Jackson repeated it and remained deep in thought. It wasn't so deep, however, that he didn't kiss Caden's hand when the little boy reached for him. Jackson didn't take the baby, but he stayed close and tickled Caden. Caden giggled.

"So we have both Evan and Shannon lying," she commented. The serious discussion seemed totally out of place with Caden's laughter and smiles, but Bailey knew this discussion had to happen. "A coincidence?"

Jackson shrugged. "Maybe. What I need is more information, and I need to figure out if Evan, or even Ryan Cassaine, had some part in this illegal adoption."

Yes, Ryan had seemed uncomfortable as well during his visits. Did the man have something to hide?

"Who's more likely to give you the answers you need—Evan or Ryan?" she asked.

He shook his head. "I'm not sure I trust either of them anymore to tell me the truth." Still, he opened his cell and made a call.

It was Ryan Cassaine who answered. "Jackson, I was hoping you'd call so I could apologize again for Shannon demanding money—"

"Is Shannon with you right now?" Jackson interrupted.

"No. We didn't drive out to your estate together, and she left her car by your front gate. When Steven drove us back down, Shannon and I went our separate ways. Don't worry, Jackson, I'll make sure she doesn't bother you again with demands for money."

"Why did she lie?" Jackson demanded. Good. Bailey was glad that he got right to the heart of the matter.

"Lie? I don't think she's lying about the baby—"

"She is. And I have proof. What I want to know is why. Is this just about money, or is it something more?"

Ryan stayed quiet for a moment. "What do you mean by *more?*"

"I mean, are you involved in this little scheme of hers?"

"No!" Ryan jumped to answer that. "Are you sure she's lying?"

"Positive."

"But she gave you a copy of the maternity test results," Ryan reminded him.

"She, or someone else, faked them. It's as simple as that. Come on, Ryan. Do you honestly think I would take her word, or yours, that the results are legit without verifying it? And I did verify that she was lying. She's not Caden's birth mother."

More silence, and the lawyer made a sound of frustration. "I don't know what to think. You obviously believe I've done something wrong, and I haven't. When you asked me to help arrange for a private adoption, that's what I did. I put out feelers and contacted other adoption attorneys to see if they had any leads. I worked my butt off to find Caden for you."

Jackson gave an impatient huff. "I don't doubt that, but I need to know if you cut any corners."

"None," Ryan insisted. "The only mistake I made was listening to Shannon and her apparent pack of lies."

"How did you meet Shannon?" Jackson asked, taking the question right out of Bailey's mouth.

"Shannon and some of the other maternity hostages are being represented by another attorney in my firm. The hostages are suing the hospital for poor security measures. I met Shannon while she was doing some paperwork here, and that's when she confessed that she was Caden's birth mother."

Bailey shifted Caden in her arms so she could get closer to the phone. "But when you first set up the adoption, you were in contact with another woman, the student, who claimed that Caden was hers."

"Yes," Ryan readily admitted. "I didn't actually meet her, though, and I never spoke directly with her. I dealt with her attorney, Phillip Dalkey."

"I want his number," Jackson demanded.

"I can give it to you, but it won't do any good. I've been trying to contact him for two days, and he's not answering his phone. His office insists they don't know where he is."

Oh, mercy. Did this Phillip Dalkey have a run-in with the person who'd hired those gunmen, or was Ryan lying about this as well?

"Go back four months ago," Jackson continued. "You said you put out feelers to find a baby for my private adoption. Was it Phillip Dalkey who first contacted you about Caden?"

Ryan made a sound to indicate he was giving that some thought. "No. Actually, it was someone else, someone we both know."

"Shannon?" Jackson asked, his voice loaded with sarcasm.

"Not Shannon either. The person who called to tell me about Caden was your business manager, Evan Young."

Chapter Twelve

Evan.

Jackson didn't like the way his business manager's name kept popping up in this investigation. Evan shouldn't have had anything to with the adoption; but according to Ryan, Evan had been the one who started the ball rolling when it came to finding Caden.

If Ryan was telling the truth.

After all, Ryan had actually profited from the adoption. Jackson had proof of that, since he'd paid the attorney a large amount in legal fees. As far as Jackson knew, Evan hadn't received a dime for anything related to the adoption.

Of course, maybe this wasn't about money.

"You think Evan is playing some kind of mind game with you?" Bailey asked.

She had worry written all over her face, and it shouldn't have been there. This should have been a time for celebration. For Bailey anyway. She'd found her missing baby and was holding him in her arms. Jackson figured this was the best moment of her life, and yet that moment was clouded with the possibility that the person who'd orchestrated the illegal adoption might be planning something worse.

Since both Caden and she were staring at him, Jackson went to them and gathered both in his arms. He kissed Caden's cheek and intended to do the same to Bailey. A simple, reassuring peck. But hell, he needed more than that, and judging from her expression, so did she.

So Jackson kissed her on the mouth.

He hadn't planned for it to go on, but it did. And despite the fact that Caden was right there, Jackson still felt the heat from the attraction. Even the danger couldn't make that go away.

Soon, very soon, he would have to figure out what to do about the attraction. And about Caden. He didn't think Bailey was ready to jump into a custody battle with him, but she would want to claim her son.

At that thought, Jackson pulled back and took a deep breath. Caden laughed, apparently amused with the kiss and his daddy's reaction. Jackson pressed his forehead to Caden's and hoped his son wasn't also aware that his daddy's heart was breaking.

He couldn't lose Caden.

Jackson opened his phone again and called Steven so he could ask the man to track down numbers for Shannon and the attorney, Phillip Dalkey. Normally, that would be an assignment he would give to Evan, but Jackson wanted to keep his business manager, and anyone else from the office, out of the information loop until he was sure Evan had no part in any of this. Steven assured Jackson that he would get back to him with the contact numbers as soon as possible. Jackson ended that call and made another one.

To Evan.

Evan's phone rang. And rang—five rings before it

went to voicemail. Strange. In the seven years that Evan had worked for him, Jackson couldn't remember once, not even on Christmas Eve, that the man hadn't answered on the first ring. Evan often joked that he even showered with his phone close enough to reach.

"Something's not right," Jackson mumbled.

"I agree." Bailey kept Caden close to her. "Part of me wishes they'd all just disappear. But we have to know who's behind all of this."

Yeah. And then they had to figure out how to deal with the aftermath.

Bailey stared at him, huffed and dropped her head on his shoulder. "I know what this is doing to you."

"And I know what you've been through for the past four months," Jackson countered. "Don't worry. We'll work out something."

Though he had no idea what.

He could ask Bailey to move onto the estate. There was plenty of room. That way, they could share custody. Of course, Bailey would almost certainly want full custody, and Jackson was afraid the law would be on her side, especially since the adoption wasn't final yet.

That got his mind and heart racing.

All she had to do was go to the police and tell them the DNA results. Family services would step in and probably take Caden and place him in foster care until they got this mess all sorted out. That could take months or longer.

Jackson had never felt this kind of panic before, and it shocked him when Bailey came up on her toes and kissed him.

"We'll work it out," she promised. And because Jackson desperately needed something to hang on to, he believed her.

He was about to seal that promise with another kiss, but his phone rang, and since the call was from Steven, Jackson answered it right away.

"I got the numbers for Shannon and Phillip Dalkey," Steven explained, "but neither is answering their phones."

Great. First Evan and now Shannon. Ryan had already told him that Phillip seemed to be missing, but Jackson had hoped he would get lucky.

"Robin Russo is back," Steven added. "She showed up at the gate about five minutes ago. Sir, she's practically hysterical and says someone's trying to kill her."

On most days, Jackson would have been alarmed by that, but this wasn't most days.

Welcome to the club, Robin.

"Should I let her in?" Steven asked.

Jackson didn't even have to think about it. "No. I don't want her inside the estate, and it's too cold for an outdoor meeting. Are you at the gate with her now?"

"Yes, sir."

"Then use the security camera to set up a video feed into my office." Jackson ended the call and looked at Bailey. "I doubt I'll learn anything from her—"

"I want to be there when you talk to her," Bailey insisted.

Jackson hesitated, figuring, at best, this conversation with Robin would be a waste of time, but he understood Bailey's need to get to the truth. "Come on. We'll leave Caden in the nursery with Tracy. It's time for his bath anyway."

Since Tracy was already in the nursery waiting for

them, it didn't take long for Bailey to give her Caden so they could then head to his office. By the time they arrived, Steven had already set up the video feed, and Jackson saw Robin on his laptop screen.

The woman was indeed waiting by the massive front gates. She had also gotten out of her car and was staring directly into the camera. She had her coat wrapped tightly around her and had ducked her head against the bitter winter wind. Judging from her red, swollen eyes, she'd been crying.

Jackson hit the button on his laptop that would allow two-way communication. "Robin," he greeted. "Back for round two already?"

"I'm back because I need your help." She moved even closer to the camera so that her face took up the entire screen. "Please let me in."

"You can say what you need to say right where you are," Jackson insisted.

Robin didn't get angry. She fired several glances over her shoulder as if she expected someone was about to ambush her. Jackson hoped that wasn't true, but he couldn't risk Bailey's and Caden's lives by allowing this suspect back onto the property.

"Could you get your man to leave?" Robin asked. "I don't trust him. I don't trust anyone right now."

Jackson thought about that a moment. "Is the gate locked and the security system activated?" he asked Steven.

"They are," Steven answered. "Should I go?"

Again, Jackson gave it some thought. The fence was crash-proof, something he'd never thought he would need, but he was glad he had it now. "Leave her there and drive back up the estate. I need you to keep checking those numbers for me."

For Shannon, Evan and the attorney, Phillip Dalkey. Plus, if there truly was a threat to Robin's life, Jackson didn't want Steven out there in the open.

Jackson did a split screen so he could watch as Steven got back into his vehicle and drove away. Robin didn't utter a word until the man was out of sight.

"After I left your estate, someone tried to run me off the road," Robin continued, her voice and expression a tangle of nerves. "At first I thought it was an accident. But about an hour ago, someone tried to do it again." Her mouth was trembling so hard now that it was difficult to make out her words. "If you or Bailey set someone on me, please call him off. I didn't do anything wrong."

"Neither Bailey nor I set anyone on you," Jackson let her know. "You've been to the police?"

"I just called them, and I'm going there after I leave here. But if you're behind this, I don't think San Antonio PD will be able to stop it."

Jackson and Bailey exchanged glances. Since Bailey and he knew they hadn't hired anyone to go after Robin, that meant someone else might have, or else the woman was lying.

Either was possible.

Bailey moved next to Jackson so that Robin would be able to see her on the monitor. "Maybe this is because of the house you purchased. Did you borrow the money from the wrong people?"

"No!" Robin practically shouted, but then just as quickly, the fight seemed to take everything out of her. "If you must know, I got a legal settlement with the hospital, but I signed a confidentiality statement. That's why I couldn't say where I got the money."

Convenient. That wouldn't be an easy thing to verify or disprove.

"You've come to the wrong people," Bailey explained. "Jackson and I don't want you dead."

"Well, somebody does." Robin looked over her shoulder again and swallowed hard. "Maybe it's Shannon. Maybe she's trying to kill us all."

"Why would she want to do that?" Jackson asked.

Robin opened her mouth as if she were about to blurt out something, but then she glanced around her again. Either she was a good actress, or she truly thought she was in danger just by being there.

When she turned back to the camera, her breath was uneven, and she was trembling even more than when this bizarre conversation had started.

"You're positive you're not trying to kill me?" Robin repeated.

"Positive," Jackson assured her.

She nodded and swallowed hard again. "Then it has to be Shannon."

Jackson couldn't assure her that Shannon wasn't guilty, especially after the stunt she'd pulled about saying she was Caden's biological mother.

Robin moved even closer to the camera, so close that her breath fogged-up the screen. "I think Shannon was having an affair with one of the gunmen who took the hostages."

One look at Bailey, and her shocked expression confirmed that this was something she hadn't heard before. But like the other things Shannon and Robin had said, it didn't necessarily make it true.

"Did you hear me?" Robin pressed. "Shannon was sleeping with one of the gunmen, and she probably helped him set up the entire hostage mess."

"You have proof?" Bailey asked.

Robin shook her head and the tears returned. "No. But I heard her talking about him one day. Danny Monroe. And I don't think it's a coincidence that one of the gunmen had the same name."

Jackson immediately saw a flaw in Robin's accusation. Two of them, in fact. "Why didn't SAPD find this connection, and why didn't you tell them?"

"I didn't remember until yesterday. Maybe it's the danger, but that conversation I had with her just came back to me. Here's what I think—we know that the gunmen wanted to kill Bailey that day…."

"They did," Bailey confirmed in a whisper. "They thought I'd seen them without their ski masks."

"Exactly!" Robin continued. "So I think Shannon hid you because of the baby. She didn't want her boyfriend coming after you and hurting the child."

That turned Jackson's stomach, but he couldn't dismiss that part. The mystery woman had told Bailey to keep quiet or the gunmen might try to use the baby to get to her. And by getting to her, the gunmen no doubt wanted to silence her permanently.

"So if Shannon took my baby, then why didn't she return him after the gunmen were killed?" Bailey asked.

"I'm guessing greed," Robin readily supplied. "I figure she sold the baby or something."

Jackson slipped his arm around Bailey. It was obvious this nightmare was difficult to relive.

"Robin, you should tell the police everything you just told us," Bailey insisted.

"I will, but for now I need your help to stop Shannon from trying to kill me."

"I'm not letting you in," Jackson repeated. "Leave now and go to the sheriff or SAPD."

Robin cursed, and she was still cursing when she made another glance over her shoulder. The profanity died on her lips. Her eyes widened, and she screamed.

But Robin's scream didn't drown out the loud blast. Someone had just fired a shot.

Chapter Thirteen

Bailey broke into a run, headed for the nursery. She didn't wait to see what was happening to Robin. She had to get to Caden and make sure he was safe.

Jackson was right behind her, but he had already grabbed his gun and then taken out his phone, no doubt to call and make sure no one had breached security.

"The gate's still closed," Jackson reminded her, shoving his gun into the waist of his pants.

Yes, but there could still be another attack on the estate.

Bailey raced into the nursery, and her heart dropped when she didn't see Caden. She hurried through the massive room and to the adjoining bathroom.

And there he was.

He was sitting in a yellow safety ring in the center of the bathtub. He was splashing water and laughing.

"What's wrong?" Tracy asked.

"Someone fired a shot near the gate," Jackson answered. "Go ahead and take Caden to the panic room."

Tracy had already started to do that before Jackson even finished. The nanny grabbed a thick terry cloth towel and swirled it around the soaking-wet baby.

Caden obviously didn't like having his bath interrupted, because he started to fuss and squirm.

"You should go with them," Jackson told Bailey while he still had his phone pressed to his ear.

It was tempting to be safely tucked away with her son, but she didn't want anyone breaking into the estate. Jackson would need all the backup he could get.

"I can help you keep watch," Bailey insisted. But it nearly brought tears to her eyes to see Tracy whisk Caden in the direction of the panic room. "We need to put an end to this."

Yes, it was stating the obvious. They did need to end it. But how? The only way to stop the attacks was to figure out who was behind them. Could Robin possibly help with that?

"Steven," Jackson said when the man came back on the line. "What's happening out there?" Jackson grabbed Bailey's hand and headed back to his office. The moment they were inside, he locked the door and used a keypad to engage the room's security system.

Bailey couldn't hear Steven's response, but she could see the security monitors when they got to his desk. He still had the split-screen images, and on the one by the gate, she saw the car speeding away. Robin's car perhaps.

But Bailey didn't see the shooter.

Jackson took out his handgun, put it on the desk and typed in something on his keyboard. He pulled up six more images on the screen. Both of them moved closer, examining the various camera angles.

"I don't see anyone either," Jackson relayed to Steven. "Maybe the person followed Robin. Call the sheriff so he can get someone out there on the road to protect her."

Of course, it might be too late for that. Robin could already be dead. And if so, the shooter might come back to the estate.

"Make certain everything is locked up tight," Jackson told Steven. "No one is getting in or out of the estate until the sheriff has the shooter in custody."

Jackson ended the call and sank down behind his desk so he could continue to scan the security feed. Bailey's heart was pounding now, and the adrenaline was raging through her. Her body was preparing itself for a fight. A fight she prayed wouldn't be necessary.

"What do we do?" she asked.

"We wait. Steven and his men will patrol the grounds and make sure no one gets onto the property. Then we let the sheriff do his job. It wouldn't be smart for me to go out there and leave Caden and you here."

"I agree." There was no way she would let Jackson leave. She was still recovering from the last time he'd done that, and they hadn't been—well—as close as they were now.

The stakes were so much higher on many levels.

Bailey sat on the armrest of his chair so she could have a better view of the computer screen. And so she could be near Jackson. It was stupid, but just being near him made her feel safer. He must have sensed that, because he slipped his arm around her and drew her closer.

There. She felt it. That click in her head that turned off some of the adrenaline rush. Her breathing began to slow down. She wondered if Jackson knew just how much he could soothe her with a mere touch.

For now, anyway.

It was highly probable they had their own personal storm brewing over Caden. Would they be enemies before this was over? Bailey hated the thought of never being able to sit with him like this again, but she had to put her baby first. She'd already lost so much time with Caden, she wouldn't let anyone, including Jackson, rob her of another day.

She forced her attention back on the screen, but there were still no signs of attack. Steven and some of the men were moving around outside, and they were all armed, bracing themselves for the worst.

Thankfully, the worst didn't seem to be coming.

"I think Caden and Tracy should stay in the panic room," Jackson mumbled. "He'll be ready for a nap soon anyway, and he can take it in there."

Bailey couldn't argue with that. The panic room was the safest place to be.

"Are you all right?" Jackson asked.

She looked over at him to see what had prompted that question and noticed he was staring at her.

"It'll be okay," he added.

Of course, Bailey knew he couldn't possibly guarantee that, but again, it made her feel good just to hear it.

She was obviously in big trouble here.

In the past two days, people had tried to kill them and kidnap Caden. A woman had been shot at just minutes earlier. But she couldn't stop feeling all warm and comforted because of Jackson.

With his attention fastened back onto the screen, he took her hand, brought it to his mouth and brushed his lips over her skin. "It'll be okay," he repeated.

"I don't know how," she mumbled.

Jackson kept hold of her hand. "You have to trust that we can get through this and work out everything. We're not enemies, Bailey. Far from it," he added.

Was that true? Yes, there was this attraction that seemed to be getting hotter and heavier every time they were together. Or apart. Heck, it just kept growing, even when they needed to focus all their attention on other things.

"We can't work this out in bed," she added.

He glanced up, and the corner of his mouth lifted. "No. But we can work out plenty of other things there."

That smile nearly melted her.

She shook her head. "I don't understand this."

"Simple." Jackson touched his mouth to her hand again. "You're a beautiful woman and I want you. That's all there is to it."

"Really?" she questioned. "Caden isn't part of this?"

"No," he said with complete conviction.

Jackson's phone rang, the sound slicing through the awkward silence.

"It's Steven," Jackson said after glancing at the caller ID screen.

Maybe this was the good news she'd been praying for. Maybe Steven or the sheriff had caught the person who fired the shot at Robin.

"Interesting," Jackson said, after at least a minute of silence. Another minute passed. "Dig into the accusation Robin made about Shannon being involved with one of the gunmen who took the hostages. Danny Monroe is the name. Let me know if you learn anything."

Jackson hung up and looked at her. "Steven has someone reviewing all the security feed, and he's not convinced there is a gunman."

"What? But we heard the shot."

"Yeah," Jackson agreed. "But remember, Robin kept moving close to the camera so we couldn't see what was going on around her."

Of course. Bailey had thought that was because the woman only wanted Jackson and her to hear what she was saying. "You think Robin could have set this all up and fired the shot herself?"

He shrugged. "It's possible. Maybe this was her plan, so we'd no longer be suspicious of her. She could be trying to gain our sympathy and trust."

And it nearly worked. Bailey had indeed been terrified for Robin's safety. Now she was riled to the core that Robin would try to manipulate them that way.

"Steven's already called the sheriff and SAPD," Jackson added, and his phone rang again. "It's Evan." He opened the phone and put it on speaker. "I tried to reach you."

"Yes, I got your message." And that's all he said for several moments. "I was out of the office when you called."

"Obviously." Jackson paused, too. "I wanted to ask you a couple of things. First, why did you have the lab fake the results of the DNA test?"

"Who said I did?" Evan immediately countered.

"Me. I know they're fake because I ran another set."

Evan cursed. "You didn't trust me?"

"No. And apparently my instincts were right."

"I did it to protect you," Evan insisted. "I didn't want you to lose Caden."

"That wasn't your call to make," Jackson insisted. "Now, talk to me about Ryan Cassaine. He said you're the one who told him about the college student who wanted to put up her baby for adoption."

"Yes, it was me. What about it?"

"Well, considering that I now know there are some questionable aspects about Caden's adoption—"

"Wait a minute," Evan interrupted. "You think I had something to do with stealing Bailey Hodges's baby?"

"Did you?" Bailey demanded.

"No." A moment later, Evan cursed and repeated his adamant denial. "I can't believe I have to defend myself like this. Jackson told me he wanted to adopt a baby, so I started asking around. This lawyer called out of the blue. Phillip Dalkey. And he said he had a client who might be willing to give up her child, but that she would need compensation. So I called Ryan and gave him the contact info. That's all. That's the only part I played in all this."

"And it has nothing to do with your fiancée's death?" Bailey prompted.

"No. Jackson, please tell me you don't believe any of this."

"I don't want to believe it, but I have to check out all the angles. Someone sent a man here to kill Bailey and me and kidnap Caden. I have to make sure that everyone around me is someone I can trust."

"Bailey's around you," Evan snapped.

"Yes, because I trust her. She has as much to lose here as I do."

"And she has everything to gain. That includes her son and your money." Evan's words were rushed now, and laced with bitterness. "Have you ever considered that she might have been the one to set up the illegal adoption? Bailey gets a cool million for turning over her baby to you, temporarily, and then a few months later she comes to the estate with DNA results and a sob story about someone stealing her baby. She takes Caden. It's a win-win for her."

Bailey frantically shook her head and turned to Jackson to defend herself, but Jackson gently tightened the grip he had on her.

"If Bailey had been trying to scam me, she would have showed up weeks ago. And she damn sure wouldn't have hired a gunman who'd get so close to Caden."

Bailey still held her breath. She couldn't afford to have Jackson think she was guilty of anything, because he might toss her out. God knows how long it would take for her to get Caden then.

"You'll lose Caden to her," Evan said a moment later.

"Probably. Merry Christmas, Evan. We'll talk after the holidays." Jackson closed his phone and dropped it onto his desk.

"Probably," Bailey repeated under her breath. She certainly hadn't expected that admission from Jackson.

Here she'd been trying to mentally prepare herself for a custody battle with one of the richest men in the country, and that "probably" had sounded like...surrender.

And it touched Bailey the way nothing else could have.

Jackson loved Caden. She was positive of that. Just

as positive as she was that Caden loved Jackson. Yet, that "probably" meant he was at least willing to consider losing the child he loved.

"I didn't come here to scam you," she reminded him.

But Jackson waved her off before she even finished. "I know."

He stood, pulling her to her feet. In the same motion, he drew her into his arms. "Evan's on the back burner for now. If he's the one behind this, then eventually he'll try to strike again. He won't succeed, with all the security precautions we've put in place. Eventually, he or the person responsible will be caught."

The idea sounded so simple. So convincing. And maybe that's why Bailey didn't pull back and launch them into a conversation that neither of them was anxious to have. Or maybe she just stayed there because it felt good to have him hold her.

"Can we get Caden from the panic room?" she asked. But she still didn't move out of his arms.

"Soon." Jackson didn't let go either. He held her and kissed the top of her head.

The air changed between them. Or something changed. Maybe it was all happening inside her and had nothing to do with the air. Bailey didn't care. She only wanted this moment and all the feelings that came with it.

It wasn't exactly hot passion that sent her in search of his mouth. Something else was going on here. Something that seemed to go bone-deep. Maybe deeper. Something that stirred her heart and blood even more than this fierce attraction could have.

She was falling hard for Jackson Malone.

That was it. More than the fire in her blood, there were the flames in her heart. It was probably stupid to fall for a man like him. A man who could cost Bailey her son and everything else. But her heart wasn't going to let her back out of this. In fact, her heart was the part of her that urged her to kiss him. Really kiss him—until any doubts that she had simply melted away.

"You're sure?" she heard Jackson ask.

Bailey didn't even have to think about this. She had never been more certain of anything in her life.

Chapter Fourteen

Jackson wasn't sure about this at all.

The timing was all wrong, but then the timing had sucked ever since Bailey had come into his life. They had so many things to work out—and he'd already insisted they wouldn't be able to work them out in bed—but here they were, heading in that direction.

Well, in the direction of his desk anyway.

Judging from the heat of the kiss she had initiated, they wouldn't make it out of his office, much less all the way to the bedroom.

He forced himself to think of the consequences, but those consequences kept getting bogged down in the hazy passion that was slamming hard and fast through his body. He blamed that on Bailey's kiss. On the way her breasts were brushing against his chest. Everything seemed to be coming down to sex, and it didn't seem to matter if Jackson wasn't convinced that sex should happen.

"This is more than I thought it would be," Bailey mumbled against his mouth.

Her words made it through the haze somehow, and he shook his head trying to figure out what she meant.

More than sex?

Jackson was about to stop, to tell her that it couldn't be more. They had too much to work out. Too much to do. Hell, someone was trying to kill them, or at least make them believe that. Life was so far from perfect that *perfect* didn't even seem to be on their radar.

Did that stop him from kissing her?

No.

He deepened the already too-deep kiss and tightened his grip around her. He slid his hand between them so he could cup her breast.

"I'm falling for you," Bailey whispered.

Even though her voice barely had sound, he heard it loud and clear. And that caused him to stop.

Jackson pulled back and stared down at her, trying to figure out what he could possibly say to that. Her words were like red flags because of his old wounds and baggage. He'd spent years avoiding words like that. Years making sure that no one ever got close enough to hurt him again.

Bailey's warm breath hit his mouth. Her eyes were half closed. Dreamy. And waiting. Either he had to dive right into this or step back. Stepping back was in his comfort zone. Years of practice had made it almost a rote response.

Don't get too close.

But this was Bailey. Hadn't he known from the moment they'd met that nothing between them would ever be ordinary?

"If you want to stop…" she whispered.

He laughed, but there wasn't an ounce of humor in it. "The last thing I want to do is stop. I want you more than my next breath."

She nodded, as if that was all there was to this. She

slid her hand around the back of his neck and pulled him in for another kiss.

"Later, we'll deal with the *later*," she said, just as her mouth touched his. That simple touch shot through him, turning his body into a furnace all over again.

Later would no doubt be harder than hell, but it would be easier than resisting her now. Jackson knew he stood zero chance of that. So he just took charge and went with it. When *later* came around, he would accept the responsibility for letting his heart and libido rule his head.

Jackson kissed her, and he didn't hold anything back. He put all of his feelings, his frustration and the white-hot heat into that kiss. And he didn't stop there. The need had already made him crazy, so he decided to make Bailey crazy right along with him.

He dropped test kisses on her neck and listened for her response. She moaned when he got to the base of her neck, so he lingered there long enough to please her and himself.

She tasted like all of the best parts of Christmas.

If the need hadn't been driving him to speed things up, he would have taken more time to savor her, to watch her respond to the kisses that he trailed down her neck and to the tops of her breasts. But this wasn't a simmering fire. It was a full blaze for both of them.

Jackson pushed down the top of her stretchy dress. Pushed down her lacy bra. Maybe the *later* part would involve a second round so he could taste and sample and touch every part of her. But for now, he settled for wetting his fingers in his mouth and circling her right nipple.

She moaned, arched her back. The change in positions

sent her sex pushing against his. Jackson was already hard and ready to take her, but that was just a reminder that the taking couldn't wait.

Bailey began to fight with her clothes, shoving up her dress and then going after his zipper. Yeah, the heat was making them crazy and speeding up everything until it was a blur. But what he was feeling wasn't a blur. The need just kept slamming into him, until all he could do was pull her to the floor.

Later, he would apologize for taking her like a sex-starved teenager.

The moment her back was on the floor, Bailey reached for him, pulling him onto her. The location and the timing no longer seemed important. Nothing did, except for what was about to happen.

Jackson kept kissing her, hoping that her taste would satiate him enough so he would slow down. No such luck. Her taste and her eager hands just fueled the already-raging heat, and when he found the top of her panties, he peeled them off her.

He had to touch her. Couldn't resist. So, as he'd done with her breasts, he eased his fingers inside her. Into all that slick heat that was a primal invitation to his aroused body.

Bailey obviously thought turnabout was fair play. She unzipped him and took him into her hands. Jackson could have sworn his eyes crossed, and he heard himself curse. The need was shouting for him to take her *now now now,* but, man, he wanted this to last for hours.

Lasting hours was obviously a pipe dream.

He drew back his hand and entered her slowly. Or rather, that's what he tried to do. But Bailey made the intimate contact complete by lifting her hips.

Whatever was better than Christmas, this was it.

Any coherent thought that was left in his head was toast now. He was beyond thinking, and he moved inside Bailey, taking them both to the only place their bodies needed to go.

She made a sound of pure pleasure. A sound Jackson was positive he would never forget. He wouldn't forget that look on her face either. Part relief, part surprise.

All Bailey.

Her hands were frantic, reaching for him, dragging him closer, even though getting closer wasn't possible. There was a flicker of panic in her eyes, as if she thought for just a split second that she wasn't going to get the relief she needed.

But she came in a flash.

Jackson didn't stop. He was already too close to taking the leap himself, but that didn't prevent him from savoring the incredible woman in the throes of her orgasm.

It was Bailey who drew him deeper into her. Bailey who urged him on. Bailey who took him right over that cliff with her.

The French were right. It was a little death. Everything slammed toward that one moment. That overwhelming moment where everything became crystal clear. Where everything was reborn. And in that moment Jackson could see and feel only one thing.

Bailey.

He whispered her name as he buried his face against her neck and let himself go.

Jackson tried to move, to readjust their positions so that he wasn't crushing Bailey, but his body seemed reluctant to break the intimate connection. He finally managed to roll to the side, but he kept her in his arms. She rolled right along with him, and they landed on their sides and face-to-face.

Somehow, this was more intimate than when he'd been inside her.

Jackson considered himself a strong, occasionally ruthless man, but Bailey had a way of bringing him to his knees.

He wanted to tell her that she was beautiful and that what had just happened was pretty damn amazing. But he heard the ringing sound. For a moment, Jackson thought it was all in his head.

It wasn't.

It was his cell.

He hated the interruption, but since this could be a critical call from Steven or the sheriff, he reached up to the desk and answered the phone.

The caller ID flashed Captain Shaw Tolbert.

Jackson knew the name. Tolbert was a bigwig in the San Antonio Police Department, and that meant the captain might have news about the gunmen and the investigation.

Jackson took the call while he helped Bailey up from the floor. He sandwiched the phone between his ear and shoulder so he could talk while he fixed his clothes.

"Captain Tolbert," Jackson greeted. Judging from Bailey's suddenly alert expression, this was a conversation she wanted to hear, so Jackson put it on speaker. "What can I do for you?" But Jackson was hoping it was the other way around, and that the captain would help end this danger breathing down their backs.

"I got a call from your estate manager and he told me about the latest attack. Or the ruse, if that's what it turns out to be. We're looking into the matter. And we're looking for Robin Russo because she's still a suspect in the disappearance of Bailey Hodges's baby."

Jackson and Bailey exchanged glances. While it was a glance on her part, since she was putting her panties back on, Jackson did more than glance. Then he forced his attention back to the phone call. "And what about Shannon Wright?"

"Also a suspect. Both women were in the hospital the day of the hostage crisis, and both have some critical time gaps that they can't or won't account for. I also understand Robin accused Shannon of having an affair with one of the gunmen." The captain groaned softly. "We thought this case was over four months ago, when SAPD killed the gunmen who took the hostages. But things have happened. There have been other attacks."

"So I've heard. And witnessed firsthand. Twice, someone has come after Bailey while she's been at my estate. What I want to know is, is Shannon or Robin responsible for that?"

"We're not sure. Either or both could be innocent. We have no proof that Shannon and the gunman, Danny Monroe, were involved romantically or otherwise. We had her followed after the hostage incident ended, and she never met with Danny. There were no calls to him either, according to her cell phone records."

"So why would Robin accuse Shannon of something like that?" Jackson asked.

"Maybe to throw suspicion off herself," the captain suggested. "There are things going on. We've gotten wind of another possible hostage situation."

"Oh, God." Bailey pressed her fingers to her mouth, but it didn't suppress the sound of her words.

"Is that Miss Hodges?" Captain Tolbert asked.

"Yes." Her voice was shaky now, and Jackson knew why. She didn't want anyone else to go through the nightmare that she'd experienced.

"We're working with another hostage, a woman we're calling hostage number four, so that the media doesn't plaster her identity all over the press," the captain continued. "She has some memory loss, but we're hoping we can unleash those memories so she can tell us more about what happened in the hospital four months ago. Anything *you* can tell us?"

Bailey shook her head and inched closer to the phone. "No. I had just had a C-section when the gunmen came into the ward. I didn't know anything about it until after the fact. Until after my baby had been taken."

The captain stayed quiet a moment. "Someone's trying to kill this other hostage, too," he revealed. "That's why it's important that we get to the bottom of Shannon's or Robin's possible involvement."

"Both of them are liars," Jackson volunteered, "so I seriously doubt you'll get the truth from them."

"You're probably right, but I want to reinterrogate both women. I'm hoping your sheriff can locate Robin since we know she was just out at your place. But do you have any idea where Shannon is?"

"None," Jackson answered. "She came to the estate with some bogus papers and claimed she was my adopted son's biological mother. She's not. Bailey is."

Bailey expected the captain to jump right on that, but he calmly said, "I see. Well, that's resolved. And the baby is safe?"

Not really. But Jackson would remedy that.

"Someone sent a man out to kidnap him and probably kill Jackson and me as well," Bailey blurted out.

"Yes, Sheriff Gentry gave me an update on that. The guy's name was Melvin Cross, a hired gun. He was a big badass years back, but his love of the bottle put him off his game. He's been off our radar for nearly a decade."

So that meant someone could have hired him cheap. It also meant this drunken SOB could have harmed Caden by accident rather than design. Not that he needed it, but it gave Jackson even more reason to go after the person who was behind all of this.

"Talk to me about these threatening letters you've received," the captain said to Jackson.

Those. It was yet something else on his too-full plate. "I got another one yesterday morning. Someone left it outside my downtown office, but it was left in an area where there were no security cameras."

"Yeah, that's what the detective handling it told me. You think that threat is connected to everything else that's going on?"

"I have no idea." And he didn't. "But it can't be a coincidence."

"Well, we're looking into it," the captain explained, "because it might be connected. It's true, none of your security cameras were aimed in that area, but we're trying to tap into the ATM camera of the bank just up the street. We might get lucky."

Yes, but even if they identified the person who'd left it, Jackson couldn't see how it would be part of the attempts to kill him and kidnap Caden. A threatening letter was benign compared to those other attempts.

"What happens now?" Bailey asked the captain.

"We keep working with hostage number four, and we help her regain her memory. And get her to trust us. Things aren't going so well in that department," Captain Tolbert added in a mumble. "In the meantime, I'll keep pressing Shannon and Robin, because I damn sure don't want another hostage incident."

No. Neither did Jackson.

"You should interrogate my business manager, Evan Young," Jackson suggested. "He also tried to fake the DNA evidence for Bailey's son. I doubt he had anything to do with the original hostage incident, but he might have learned something from Shannon after the fact."

"Thanks for the tip. I'll get him in here today, right after I talk with Ryan Cassaine."

"Ryan Cassaine?" Bailey and Jackson repeated at the same moment.

"Yeah. I just had him brought into headquarters for questioning," the captain confirmed.

Jackson was having some doubts about the adoption attorney's innocence, but it surprised him to hear that the SAPD captain was having doubts as well.

"Why did you bring in Ryan?" Jackson asked. "Is it because he cut some corners when he handled the adoption?"

"No, but I will ask him about that. Right now, I want to speak to him about his relationship with Shannon. I've just learned that they're involved romantically."

Jackson cursed. "Yeah. He brought her to the estate when she told that lie about being Caden's birth mother."

"Well, that doesn't surprise me, but what I did find

surprising was that, according to a couple of witnesses, the relationship isn't a new one."

"What do you mean?" Bailey asked.

"According to my detectives, Ryan and Shannon have been seeing each other for a while now—even before the hostage incident at the maternity hospital. Now, I need to find out just how deep the adoption attorney is into this."

Chapter Fifteen

Bailey tried to pretend that everything was normal.

In some ways, it was easy to do. After all, she was spending time with her baby. She was literally holding Caden in her arms and reading to him. She'd dreamed about moments like this, and now she had them.

But for how long?

She tried to push aside that troubling question, and continued to read the Christmas book aloud. He was too young to understand the story itself, but he slapped at the colorful pages and babbled when he saw something that caught his attention.

From the other side of the nursery, Jackson smiled at the baby's antics, but the smile was too brief, because he immediately jumped back into his phone call. Bailey had lost count of how many calls there had been, but Jackson had been working hard to get updates on the case. No easy feat, considering the investigation was now splintered between Sheriff Gentry's office, SAPD and, apparently, another set of detectives who were trying to track down and protect the other hostage with the memory issues.

Jackson had been filling Bailey in as he ended each of the outgoing and incoming calls, but the bottom line was that no one had found Shannon or Robin, and both Evan and Ryan were still insisting they were innocent.

They were back to square one.

Except that she now had her son.

Despite the danger, it was hard to be pessimistic. Soon, her son would get to experience his very first Christmas, and even the investigation couldn't put a damper on that.

However, she couldn't say the same for Jackson.

Each call seemed to frustrate him even more than the last, and it couldn't help when every time he glanced in her direction, he saw her with Caden. It had to be tearing him apart to know that he might lose the baby he loved. And there were no doubts in her mind that Jackson loved Caden with all his heart.

"Still no sign of Shannon or Robin," Jackson relayed when he ended the call with Sheriff Gentry. "SAPD questioned Ryan and Evan, but they didn't have any evidence to hold either of them."

Yes, he was frustrated, and it was just as apparent in his tone as it was in his expression. Bailey decided to do something about it.

She put the book aside, stood, and with Caden in her arms, she went to Jackson. "Come on. Let's go to the foyer and see the Christmas tree."

He shrugged as if he might refuse, but then Caden reached out for him. Bailey let her son go into Jackson's waiting arms.

"You're right," Jackson said, giving Caden a kiss on the cheek. "He should see the Christmas tree. And tonight, after he's asleep, I can take his presents out of my office closet. There are about a dozen of them crammed in there."

She was betting it was more than that. It was clear Jackson had been planning this holiday for a long time.

"After he's in bed we can talk," Jackson added, as they headed down the stairs.

Uh-oh. Bailey knew what that talk was about—custody of Caden. Maybe they would even discuss the fact that they'd had sex—and what that meant.

If anything.

Bailey's body was still humming from the experience, but she had to accept that once was all she might get with Jackson. When the investigation, the danger and the custody were all resolved, he would almost certainly remain in Caden's life, but not necessarily hers.

And if so, that would break her heart.

"See the lights?" Jackson said to Caden.

"Ooo," Caden babbled, pointing to the tree. There were indeed lights to see. Hundreds of them, and they glittered and twinkled from top to bottom, the sparkles dancing off the glass ornaments and tinsel. Someone had obviously finished the decorating and cleaned up the lights she'd broken.

It was perfect now.

Jackson and she had met by this tree, and that alone made it special, but the magical look in her son's eyes made this a moment Bailey would never forget. One glance at Jackson, and she realized he felt the same. But with a twist. He was no doubt wondering if this would be the one and only Christmas he would have with Caden.

Bailey wanted to start the discussion regarding

custody. Maybe they should just have it here and now, but then Caden babbled more of those precious sounds and waggled his fingers at the tree. Jackson took him closer for a better look.

Jackson's phone rang—again. The irritation flashed through his eyes, but because he had no choice, he handed Caden back to Bailey, took out the phone, glanced at the screen and then answered it.

"The police are looking for you, Shannon," he greeted the caller.

Shannon? So she'd turned up after all, just in time to spoil this moment with Caden and his first Christmas tree.

"You should go to SAPD," Jackson added. "They want to talk to you." He clicked the speakerphone button and held out the cell so that Bailey would be able to hear.

"I know, and when I was on the way to the police station, someone tried to run me off the road. I swear, someone's trying to kill me."

"Trust me, you're not the only one," Jackson mumbled in frustration. Unfortunately, Bailey felt the same. She wasn't just frustrated. She was weary from the attacks and the danger. She only wanted a little bit of normalcy.

"I want to come to the estate so we can talk," Shannon insisted.

Bailey shook her head, praying that Jackson would refuse, but it was obvious he didn't intend to grant Shannon's request. "We can talk now, on the phone," Jackson let the woman know, "but I'm not letting you come here. Not a chance."

Good. Bailey didn't want any of their suspects near the estate.

"I'm sorry I lied about your son being mine," Shannon continued, her voice weepy. "I was desperate, you see. I owe a lot of people money."

"So you conspired with Ryan to extort that money from me?" Jackson asked point-blank.

"No. Ryan had no part in this, I swear."

"And coming from you, that means a lot," Jackson said sarcastically. "Ryan is your lover, so I figure he'll do anything you ask."

"You're wrong. He's an honest man. The only mistake he made was getting involved with me."

Shannon sounded as if she was telling the truth, but the woman had told so many lies that Bailey wasn't about to believe her now.

"You're not denying that Ryan's your lover?" Jackson asked, pressing her.

"No, but I doubt he'd want me to confess that to anyone, especially you. He's trying to distance himself from me. And he should. I'm bad news. I can't seem to keep myself away from the wrong people."

Bailey couldn't agree more. The woman was indeed bad news. But had she really orchestrated a baby snatching and an illegal adoption?

"Talk to me about your involvement with the hostage gunman, Danny Monroe," Jackson continued.

Bailey thought she heard Shannon gasp. "Who told you I was involved with him?"

"Robin," he readily admitted.

Bailey wished she could see Shannon's face, because the woman's silence was causing Bailey to be even more suspicious of her.

"Robin," Shannon snarled. "You know why she's doing this, right?" But she didn't wait for an answer. "She wants to make me look guilty."

"Did you have an affair with Danny Monroe?" Jackson demanded.

"No. It was Robin who was having the affair. Not me."

Bailey huffed. She wanted to lock Robin and Shannon in a room and make them argue it out until they finally told the truth.

"Robin had the affair?" Jackson repeated. He was obviously skeptical.

"Yes. But I know you don't believe it. That's okay. Just stop Robin. When she's stopped, her lies will stop, too." And with that, Shannon hung up.

"I need to give Shannon's number to the SAPD," Jackson said immediately. He scrolled through his list of recent calls. There were so many of them. And he located Captain Shaw Tolbert. He pressed redial.

"Mr. Malone." The captain answered on the first ring.

"Shannon Wright just phoned me, and here's where you can reach her." Jackson read off the numbers. "She also admitted to having an affair with Ryan Cassaine."

"Thanks—I'll get someone right on that." He paused. "I'm glad you called. I needed to speak to you anyway. There's been a development in the case."

Bailey slowly drew in a breath and tried not to jump to any bad conclusions. Unfortunately, the captain's tone made that impossible. He didn't sound as if he had good news to relay.

"Remember I told you we were trying to use the

security cameras up the street from your office to determine who had left that threatening letter?"

"Yeah, I remember," Jackson said cautiously. "Did you find anything?"

"We got some images. The tech enhanced them and cleaned them up, and a few minutes ago, he managed to ID the person responsible." The captain paused again. "It was one of our suspects, Robin Russo."

JACKSON CHECKED HIS MESSAGES again to see if he had an update about Robin and her whereabouts. He didn't. And that made his temper boil to the point of exploding.

Robin better have a damn good excuse for leaving that letter, but what excuse could there be?

None.

Unless this was some kind of sick game. Pretend she was the one in trouble. Lie like crazy. And then leave him threatening letters. Hell, he could probably add baby-snatching to her list of wrongdoing.

No matter which way he looked at it, Robin Russo couldn't be trusted and could be dangerous.

And that's the reason Jackson had his laptop on the table next to him. He was using a split screen so he could easily check all the security cameras. Steven and his men were doing the same, and all of them had set their monitors to show any detection of motion. Any movement outside should register and alert them all.

Hopefully, their vigilance and the new security measures would pay off.

The grounds were lit up with both the Christmas decorations and the security lights. There was a light, misty rain falling, and it made the lights glitter even more. Everything looked festive. But the heavy illumination was also another precaution. Even if someone managed to get past the motion detectors, it wouldn't be long before someone saw them.

Jackson put away his phone and glanced first at Caden, who was sleeping in his crib, then at Bailey. She was sleeping, too. *Finally.* She was curled up on the comfy sofa in the nursery, but the blanket Jackson had draped over her earlier was now halfway to the floor, proving that her sleep was restless at best.

Neither Jackson nor she had wanted to leave Caden, so they'd agreed to stay put, with Jackson in a recliner next to the crib, and Bailey on the sofa a few feet away.

Jackson thought about joining her there. It would be a tight fit, just the right amount of space for cuddling. His body was begging for that, but it was also begging for more. If he got onto that sofa with Bailey, it wouldn't be just for cuddling.

They'd have sex.

No. They'd make love, he mentally corrected himself.

And even though he was aroused by just looking at her, Jackson understood the difference. Being with Bailey couldn't be casual. It couldn't be temporary. So it was best to sort out his feelings before…before anything else happened between them.

He checked the time. It was just past midnight, and that meant it was finally Christmas. This wasn't exactly the way he'd envisioned his first Christmas with his son, but at least Caden was here with him. Considering everything that'd happened, that was a holiday gift he was extremely grateful to have.

Jackson got up and gave Bailey's blanket an adjustment. He kept his movements light, hoping she would stay asleep, but she stirred anyway.

Her eyelids fluttered open and she looked at him. Not a startled where-am-I? look. She smiled as if his face was exactly what she'd wanted to see.

Man, that didn't help his begging body.

Nor did it help when she reached out and slid her hand around the back of his neck. Bailey pulled him to her for a kiss.

"Hmmm," she mumbled against his mouth. "Merry Christmas."

Everything about that moment, that kiss and her words, seemed so right. She was welcoming him home, right into her arms. And even though Jackson knew they should talk first and kiss later, that's not what happened.

He pulled her closer and returned the kiss, as if Bailey was his for the taking.

"Caden's asleep?" she asked, glancing over his shoulder.

Jackson nodded. Caden was asleep and would almost certainly stay that way through the entire night. That cleared a path to sex with Bailey that didn't need any more clearing.

"We'll talk later," she murmured.

Had she read his mind? Maybe she had just sensed his hesitation. But that suggestion of "we'll talk later" zapped what little hesitation he had left.

Jackson hooked his arm around her and pulled her to him. If he was going to make a mistake by being intimate with her, then he sure as hell intended to make it a mistake worth remembering.

He angled her back farther. And farther. Until she pulled him down onto the sofa and onto her. Jackson was getting ready to take this to the next level and indulge in some foreplay.

But his phone vibrated.

Jackson silently cursed. He had turned off the ringer so the sound wouldn't wake Caden, but the buzzing was still audible.

They froze, both of them obviously trying to pull themselves from the hazy passion, but Jackson didn't delay. The buzzing sound was also a reminder that all calls could be critical.

Especially this one.

"Steven," he whispered, answering the cell. Jackson got up from the sofa and went to the other side of the room.

Bailey got up as well, and with her face showing her concern, she followed him.

"Check screen six," Steven instructed.

That sent Jackson racing back across the room to the table that held his laptop. His attention went right to screen six, just as Steven had directed.

This was the back section of the property, where there was a pond and shrubs covered in Christmas lights. Jackson moved closer to the screen, trying to pick through the landscape and decorations.

"Hell," he mumbled under his breath.

Jackson spotted something.

Or rather some*one*.

Chapter Sixteen

From the moment Jackson answered Steven's call, Bailey's heart had started pounding. It was too late for this to be a casual, how-are-you check-in; and since Jackson had been getting message and text updates throughout the night, this call meant something out of the ordinary had happened.

"There," Jackson said, pointing to the spot on the screen.

Even with him pointing, it still took her a moment to see what had put the alarmed expression on his face.

There was someone scaling the fence.

Oh, God. Not again.

The person was dressed all in black and blended right into the night. In fact, if it hadn't been for the multicolored Christmas lights, she might not have seen him at all. But she did see him, and she saw the rifle he was carrying.

"I have someone on the way to intercept him," Steven explained. "The house is locked down and every inch of it wired, in case someone tries to break in. I'll call when I have more info."

Jackson shut his phone and reached for the intercom button on the wall. "Tracy?" he said.

When the nanny answered, Jackson told her to get to the nursery immediately, but Bailey didn't wait for Tracy to arrive. She gathered up Caden in his blanket so he would be ready to go. Her son obviously didn't appreciate being awakened, because he started to fuss.

Jackson made another call, to someone on his staff, and he told everyone to go to their panic room. He also called the sheriff and asked him for assistance. Maybe, just maybe, that would be enough to stop whatever was happening.

Bailey tried to console Caden by kissing his cheek and gently rocking him, but perhaps the child could feel the tension in her body. Even though Steven seemed to have this situation under control, she couldn't help but be terrified for her baby's safety.

"It's just one person," Jackson reminded her. He put his arm around Caden and her.

"One desperate person," she said under her breath.

Maybe Shannon or Robin. Maybe Evan or even Ryan. But one desperate person could do a lot of damage with a rifle.

"How many men do you have out there?" Bailey asked.

"Four, including Steven. All of them are armed. Plus, we can track this person's every move with the new security system that was just installed. He won't get far."

Or maybe *she* wouldn't get far, because it very well could be a woman beneath all those dark clothes.

"Go to the panic room," Jackson insisted, the moment Tracy rushed into the room.

But he wasn't just directing the order at Tracy, Bailey realized. He was talking to her as well.

"We've been through this before, and I'd rather stay out here in case you need help," Bailey insisted right back.

She braced herself for an argument, but his attention went back to the laptop screen. Bailey saw the shadowy figure make its way through the shrubs, and each step brought it closer to a confrontation with Steven and his men.

Each step also brought the intruder closer to the house where he or she would be in firing range with that rifle.

"Go ahead to the panic room," Bailey told Tracy. "If things get worse, I'll join you."

Tracy gave a shaky nod and took Caden from her arms. Bailey gave her son several kisses, which he tried to bat away. Obviously, he was cranky and still sleepy.

Jackson kissed the baby as well, and motioned for Tracy to leave, but he kept his attention on the monitor.

"Here," he said, handing her the gun he had next to his laptop. "I'll grab another one from my office. Keep watch on the screen, and if anything happens, yell for me."

Oh, she would do that all right. Bailey didn't want this monster anywhere near the house.

She heard Jackson run down the hall toward his office, and she saw more movement on the screen. Steven and his men were forming a circle around the intruder. It shouldn't be long before they had him. Then they'd know the identity of the person who'd been making their lives a living hell.

The intruder froze. Maybe because he heard Steven. He lifted the rifle, taking aim.

Oh, God.

She prayed he didn't shoot one of the men before they could take him down.

Bailey was still praying when she heard the sound. At first she thought it was Jackson hurrying back from his office. But it hadn't come from the hall, it came from the front of the estate. It sounded as if someone had slammed a car door. Had one of the servants gone out for something? If so, Jackson wouldn't be happy about that, because he'd ordered them all to the panic room.

She glanced in the direction of the window, but it was too far on the other side of the room. If she went there to look out, she wouldn't be able to see the computer screen. Right now, the screen was critical, because it seemed as if Steven was only seconds away from reaching the intruder.

She heard Jackson's footsteps. *Finally!* Bailey didn't like him being out of sight at a time like this. She volleyed her attention between the laptop and the open door of the nursery. Waiting.

The next sound she heard, however, sent her heart to her knees.

There was a blast. Some kind of an explosion. And it seemed to rock the entire house.

Everything inside her froze for a moment. The windows hadn't broken. There didn't seem to be any signs of damage to the nursery.

"Bailey?" Jackson called out, and he raced into the room. He had a gun in each hand. "What happened?"

She shook her head, studied the images on the screen,

and it didn't take her long to find what she was looking for. There, at the back of the house, one of the utility vehicles was on fire. That was obviously the source of the explosion.

"Where's Steven?" Jackson asked, but he didn't wait for her to answer. He hurried to the computer and looked at the images.

Steven was still there, near the intruder in the dark clothes, but he'd stopped, as if trying to figure out what was going on.

Bailey was trying to figure out the same thing.

There was another deafening blast that rattled the windows and sent things falling from the walls and tables. She held onto the laptop and frantically searched the screen. It would have been impossible to miss.

Another vehicle was in flames.

"The intruder couldn't be doing this," Jackson mumbled, and he cursed. "There must be two of them."

In the back of her mind Bailey had already come to that conclusion, but hearing it spoken aloud turned her blood to ice. This wasn't a simple trespassing. And worse, it was possible the intruder had been a decoy to draw Steven and the others away from the estate.

It'd worked.

"I need you to go to the panic room," Jackson insisted, and he put one of the guns into her hands.

This time Bailey didn't intend to argue with him. She wouldn't go into the panic room itself, but she would instead stand guard outside to make sure no one got in.

"Don't do anything dangerous," she heard herself say. And she pressed a quick kiss to Jackson's lips.

She turned to run into the hall, but Bailey didn't get far.

A bullet came crashing through the nursery window.

Jackson cursed and pulled Bailey to the floor.

Hell. This couldn't be happening again. He'd taken too many precautions for this, and no one should have been able to fire shots into the house again.

The new security alarm went off, the shrieking sound piercing the room, and the cold winter wind started to howl through the gaping hole in the broken glass.

He grabbed the laptop from the table and pulled it onto the floor with them. First he had to silence the alarms so he could hear what was happening. He didn't want an intruder to use the shrill noise to cover up an actual break-in.

Jackson punched in the codes for the security system and temporarily disengaged the alarm. Only for a few seconds. Just to stop the sound. And then he rearmed the entire system so that it would alert them if another window was broken or a door opened in any part of the estate.

"Find the shooter on the screen," he told Bailey, and keeping low, he scrambled toward the window.

"Stay away from there," Bailey warned.

But he couldn't. Since the bullet had come through the window, that meant the shooter was out there, and not on the fence this time, or it would have tripped the sensors. Or it should have anyway.

"See if you can pinpoint the gunman's location for me," Jackson asked. He stood, staying to the side of the window and peeked out.

Nothing.

"I see Steven and his men but not the gunman," she said. "Oh, God, the man wearing the dark clothes is running. I think he's heading back to the fence."

He was probably getting away or creating a diversion so the shooter could get closer to the house. Had the two crossed the fence together? That would have tripped the sensors and alerted Steven, but maybe then the pair had split up. Steven and the others might not even know they were dealing with more than one intruder, but Steven had no doubt heard those blasts and the shot.

Another bullet came crashing through the window.

Jackson jumped to the side and tried to dodge the shards of glass that spewed across the room.

Yes, there were definitely two culprits.

Maybe more.

"Stay down!" Bailey shouted.

Jackson would for now; but soon, very soon, he had to return fire to keep this person from getting closer. However, he couldn't just blindly fire shots into the night, because his own men were out there.

"Where are Steven and the others?" Jackson asked Bailey. "And what about the sheriff?" But it was still too early for the sheriff to arrive. He was a good twenty, maybe twenty-five minutes out, and while it'd felt like an eternity, this ordeal was only about ten minutes old.

He glanced at her and saw she had her gaze nailed to the laptop. "Steven and one other man are running after the intruder. Two of your men are coming back toward the house."

Good. "Where are they?"

She shook her head. "Somewhere on the grounds at

the rear of the house. It's hard to tell exactly where they are."

Hell. "Hard to tell" meant he couldn't shoot and try to end this situation.

But that wasn't true for the gunman.

He sent three rounds, one right behind the other, slamming into what was left of the window.

"I need an exact location," Jackson pressed. Because the sooner he had that, the sooner he could fire, and then he could get Bailey out of there and on the way to the panic room where she belonged.

It sickened him and riled him to the core that she was in danger again. Bailey had already been through way too much to have to deal with bullets coming at her again.

"I see your men," she finally said. "They're approaching the estate from the back, where that car is still burning."

Good. That meant they weren't on the west side of the house where the shots were coming from.

"Don't get up," Jackson reminded her.

He took a deep breath, darted out from cover, and fired through the gaping holes in what was left of the window. He figured it would take a miracle for him to hit the shooter, but that wasn't what this was all about. He needed his own diversion, a way of getting the shooter to back down so it would buy Bailey some time.

Jackson fired two shots, keeping track of how much ammunition he used. He had several magazines in his pockets, but he didn't want to go bullet-to-bullet with someone hell-bent on killing them.

Four shots came tearing right at him.

He cursed and ducked back against the wall. So much for his plan of buying some time. More shots came one right behind the other.

Jackson glanced at Bailey to make sure she was okay. She wasn't. She was on the floor, shaking, and had a death grip on the gun and the laptop. However, despite the chaos all around them, she was still focusing on the computer screen.

"I see the shooter!" she shouted over the din of the bullets.

Since this guy didn't seem to be letting up, Jackson made his way back across the room and to Bailey. Somehow, he was going to have to get her into the hall despite the fact that the bullets all seemed to be landing right around the door they would have to use to make their exit.

First though, Jackson needed to try to get a visual on everyone so he didn't end up shooting the wrong person.

He kept his ear pinned to the sound of the shots so he could tell if they changed directions, and he also studied the computer monitor. He saw who he thought must be Steven. The Christmas lights helped with the illumination, but it was still night, and everyone was wearing dark clothes. From what he could tell, two of his men were definitely at the rear of the house, and they appeared to be trying to sneak up on the gunman.

"What now?" Bailey asked, her voice trembling.

Jackson was about to tell her they were moving to the panic room. Or rather, she was.

But just like that, the shots stopped.

So did Jackson's heart.

He damn sure hadn't wanted bullets coming at them,

but if the shooter was firing, they had a good idea where he was.

"The doors and windows are all locked," Jackson reminded Bailey, hoping it would help level her breathing.

Or were they?

He'd turned off the alarm after the glass had shattered. There'd only been—what?—a minute at the most between the time the first shot was fired and his cutting the sound of the alarm so he could hear if anyone broke in. Hell. He hoped someone hadn't managed to get through one of the doors or windows during that short time before he reengaged the system.

If so, Bailey and he could be ambushed.

Jackson reached up and turned off the lights. It probably wouldn't help at this point, because the shooter obviously knew where they were; but he didn't want the overhead light to make it easier for the shooter to see them if and when he got Bailey out of there.

"Come on," Jackson instructed. "Stay down and move fast. I want to get out into the hall as quickly as possible."

She pulled in a hard breath and nodded. Her eyes were wide with fear, but she didn't panic. Far from it.

"We'll protect Caden," she insisted.

Yes, they would.

"Leave the laptop," he told her.

He wanted their hands free so they could use their weapons if it became necessary. But Jackson hoped they wouldn't have to be long without another computer tied to the surveillance system. The security feed could be transferred to his phone, and he could do that as soon as he got Bailey out of there. Then, he could keep an eye on Steven and whatever was going on at the back of the estate. He could also monitor his two men, who were no doubt trying to provide some sort of backup.

Plus, there was the sheriff. The gate was closed, but the sheriff had the security codes to open it. Still, Jackson wanted to make sure where everyone was at any given moment.

Jackson helped Bailey get into a crouching position. There were no other shots. No other sounds to indicate the location of the shooter.

"Now," Jackson instructed.

He maneuvered himself so that he was behind Bailey. It was a risk because it meant she would go first into the hall. But since the bullets had come through the window, he didn't want her in the direct line of fire either.

Jackson nudged her forward, trying to hurry. The first step was to get out of the nursery and to the back stairs. From there they could reach the library, and then the panic room. Once they were there, he would force Bailey inside where she'd be safe, so he could deal with this armed SOB.

This ended tonight.

He wasn't going to allow Bailey or Caden to be in danger any longer.

"Stay down," he reminded Bailey. After all, there were windows at the front of the hall. "And once you're out there, go to the left."

She nodded and gave him one last glance over her shoulder before she darted into the hall. Jackson was right behind her. But they only made two steps before there was a sound that Jackson didn't want to hear.

A shot.

It was a loud deafening blast.

But it hadn't come from the nursery window, and there'd been no sounds of breaking glass.

None.

And Jackson knew why.

The shooter was inside the house.

Chapter Seventeen

Bailey dropped down and flattened her body on the floor in the hall.

Oh, God.

Things had just gone from bad to worse. The shot had come from inside. How the devil had this person gotten in and brought the danger so close?

She tried to keep her gun ready, but she also pulled Jackson to the floor with her.

He didn't go willingly.

Jackson was obviously looking for the shooter so he could return fire. She knew that was necessary, but Bailey didn't want him risking his life like this. No. There had to be another way. They needed to find a place to take cover so they could try to decide how to get out of this situation.

If there was a way out.

She suddenly had a terrifying thought. Or rather several of them. What if there were more than two intruders? What if they'd already neutralized Steven and his men? And what if the sheriff couldn't get onto the grounds?

Bailey was pretty sure someone would have to open

the gate for Sheriff Gentry, and without computer access there was no way Jackson or she could do that.

"The shooter's in the foyer," Jackson mumbled under his breath.

Bailey's heart dropped.

The foyer was just below them.

She lifted her head slightly. Bad idea. A bullet went slamming into the wall directly above them.

Jackson cursed and rolled her to the side until he was in front of her. He was protecting her again, and in doing so he was placing himself in grave danger.

He levered himself up and sent a single shot down into the foyer.

Bailey looked down the hall in the direction of the back stairs. She couldn't actually see the stairs from her location, but she knew they were just on the other side of the wall. Probably a good forty feet away. Of course, once they got out of the open area where they were now, the hall might actually provide them some cover.

First though, they would have to move a couple of yards, out in the open, where the shooter would easily be able to see them.

Her heart was pounding in her ears, and her hand started to shake. Bailey thought of her precious son, and she fixed Caden's face in her head. She used that to fight off the fear. She would protect him because the alternative was unthinkable. She'd lost him for four months, and she didn't intend to lose him again.

She was about to suggest to Jackson that they just make a run for the covered part of the hall.

But then she heard a different sound.

Not a shot this time, but it was a sound that tore through her worse than any bullet ever could.

She heard a baby crying.

Bailey tried to get to her feet, but Jackson jerked her back down.

"Just listen," he whispered, his voice strained and hard as the grip he had on her.

She tried to do that. Bailey tried to latch onto any information that would help them. But the only thing she could think of was getting to Caden. Her baby was in danger.

"Caden's in the panic room," Jackson reminded her.

Was he? Tracy had certainly intended to take him there, but maybe they hadn't made it. Maybe an intruder had managed to stop them and was now holding them hostage.

"It's probably a trick," Jackson added.

Before Bailey could wrap her mind around that, another bullet slammed into the wall just a few feet away. Then another. However, over the thick blasts, she could still hear the baby crying.

Bailey struggled to get up again, and she batted away Jackson's hand. He didn't give up. He grabbed her gown and dragged her back to the floor.

"That's not Caden," he insisted.

Maybe because she could see the certainty in his eyes and on his face, Bailey forced herself to listen harder. Yes, it was a baby crying all right, but she had heard Caden cry.

Those sobs didn't belong to her son.

"It's a recording," Jackson told her. "A loop. It's the same sound being played over and over."

He was right. It was a recording. And not of Caden. This was indeed a trick, and it had come very close to working. She had nearly left what little cover they had so she could race downstairs and get to the source of those baby sobs.

The relief instantly flooded through her, even as the bullets continued to come their way. But in between the shots and the recorded sounds of a baby crying, Bailey heard something else.

Footsteps.

Jackson must have heard them, too, because his gaze whipped in that direction. Not to the steps in front of them, but to the nursery behind him. My God. Had someone used a ladder to climb up and get into the room? There wasn't a way to access it from another point in the house.

The relief that Bailey had felt just seconds earlier evaporated.

In addition to the dark-clothed intruder they'd seen on the monitor, there was a gunman in the foyer and now another, perhaps in the nursery right behind them. Three of them. Unless it was one of Jackson's guards or a servant who hadn't made it to the panic rooms. One thing was for certain. They couldn't just lie there and wait to see who might be coming out of the nursery. If it was another shooter, they'd be sitting ducks.

Jackson reached up and slapped off the hall lights. It didn't plunge them into total darkness, because there were lights on below in the foyer, but hopefully it wasn't illuminated enough for the shooter to see them clearly.

The bullets continued to tear through the walls and

the stair railings, each of them robbing Bailey of what little breath she had left.

"We need to get to the back stairs," Jackson mouthed.

Yes. Away from the foyer and away from the nursery. It would also get them closer to reaching Caden. Of course, they couldn't go in the panic room, not with the threat of danger so close. But Bailey wanted to be directly in front of that panic room door so she could be a last line of defense, if it came down to it.

"Now," Jackson whispered. "Run and don't look back."

"What are you going to do?" she demanded.

"Go now!" he demanded.

Jackson levered himself up, and in the same motion, he slammed the nursery door shut. It certainly wouldn't stop bullets, but it might slow down the person they'd heard inside the room.

Bailey stayed in a crouching position, and while she tried to keep her gun ready to fire, she started down the hall.

She didn't get far.

The barrage of shots came right at them, and she dropped back down. But not Jackson. He took aim at the person in the foyer.

And fired.

The sound seemed to echo through the entire estate, but just like that, the shots stopped.

"I think I got him," Jackson said, reaching for her.

But before Jackson could take hold of her, someone opened the nursery door. It happened in a flash. Too soon for Bailey to move out of the way.

She felt someone grab her from behind and jerk her into the dark nursery.

And then that someone jammed a gun against her head.

Everything seemed to happen at once.

Jackson saw the gunman in the foyer drop, his weapons clattering to the floor. He caught a glimpse of two of his own guards who were making their way up the back steps. He also heard a siren, probably from Sheriff Gentry's vehicle.

But all of those details melted away when he saw Bailey.

There was just a flash of movement from behind her, and then she seemed to vanish. Someone had pulled Bailey into the nursery. Jackson thought it was too much to hope that it was one of his own men.

Keeping his gun lifted and aimed, Jackson bracketed his right wrist with his left hand. He walked toward the open doorway of the nursery where Bailey had disappeared.

He saw her, right in the middle of the darkness and the cold. Her pale skin gleamed like a beacon.

So did the gun.

Not hers. Bailey's weapon was on the floor.

The one that grabbed every bit of Jackson's attention was jammed right against Bailey's temple.

"The gunman's dead," one of Jackson's guards shouted from the foyer. "We're coming up."

But Jackson shook his head, hoping they would see his response and back off. He didn't want anything prompting Bailey's captor to pull that trigger.

"It's over," Jackson said to both Bailey and the armed person hiding in the shadows behind her. "The sheriff's here. So are my men. Your partner is dead, and my guards have the other one cornered on the grounds."

He hoped.

Jackson had to take a deep breath to keep his voice steady. "Put down your gun and we can talk."

Though talking was the last thing Jackson wanted to do. Right now, he just wanted Bailey safe and in his arms. That meant he first had to get her away from that armed SOB who was likely responsible for all the hell that'd been happening over the past few days.

Jackson inched closer. "Put down the gun," he repeated.

"Don't move," the gunman ordered.

And Jackson knew exactly who'd given that order.

"Evan," Jackson growled, and he fought hard to stop himself from cursing. Even though he wanted to throttle Evan for putting the gun to Bailey's head, he couldn't antagonize the man. "There's nothing you can gain from holding Bailey. Let her go."

"Oh, there's something." Evan tried to laugh, but the sound was broken and hollow.

Hell. Evan was in way over his head here, and if he decided to fight so he could escape, Bailey could be shot. Evan's gun was literally point-blank against Bailey's temple. She wouldn't survive a shot fired at that range.

"I need a car," Evan demanded. "And some cash."

Jackson moved a fraction of an inch closer, all the while keeping watch on Evan's trigger finger. "What happened to the million dollars you got from selling Caden?"

"Most of it's gone. I had to use most of it to cover up what I did."

"And what exactly did you do?" Jackson asked, fighting to keep his voice and body calm. He didn't have a clean shot because Evan had ducked down behind Bailey.

"Robin got in touch with me when she heard you were looking to adopt a baby. She was scared and thought she would be arrested, that no one would believe she was just trying to save Bailey and her son. After all, she'd been having an affair with one of the gunmen."

"So, you convinced her to turn the baby over to you." Jackson wanted to keep Evan talking so he could hopefully distract him. If Evan moved just a little to either side, he would have a clean shot.

A shot he *would* take.

He would do anything to save Bailey.

"I gave Robin money," Evan continued. "Part of the money you forked over for the adoption."

"You sold my baby." Bailey shook her head, and that caused Evan to jam the gun even harder against her skin. Bailey winced in pain.

Every muscle in Jackson's body reacted to that wince. *How dare this SOB hurt Bailey.*

"Yes, I sold him," Evan admitted. "But it had nothing to do with you or your son. This was the way I could get back at Jackson and punish him."

Bailey swallowed hard. "Why punish Jackson? He wasn't responsible for Sybil's death."

"To hell he wasn't." Evan was frantic now, and sounded on the verge of losing it completely. "It was because of Jackson she was on that plane. If he hadn't been trying to do another hostile takeover of a company, it would have never happened. Never."

"You're right," Bailey said, her voice broken but

somehow calm. "Jackson walked away from that crash. It doesn't seem fair, does it?"

Good. Bailey was playing along and trying to keep Evan from going completely berserk.

"That's why I'll go with you," Bailey continued. "We'll get the money and the car, and you can hold me hostage until you're away from the estate."

Jackson cursed despite his attempt to stop it. "No, Bailey. Don't do this."

"I have to do it. We owe Evan that much. And besides, he doesn't want to fire any more shots, because someone could get hurt."

"You can't let Evan take you from here," Jackson said through clenched teeth.

Bailey winked at him.

Jackson tried not to show any relief, but he felt a ton of it. Bailey and he were on the same page here, thank God. Pretend to cooperate but look for the first opportunity to stop this madman.

"If you hate me so much," Jackson said to him, "then why fake the DNA results?"

"Simple. I had to make you keep trusting me. What better way than for you to believe I would lie for you."

Yeah. It was a good plan. "And if all of this blew up in your face, then you could lie to the cops and tell them that I faked the DNA results."

"Good plan, huh?" Evan said with some amusement.

Right. A good plan. The plan of a sick mind. "What about the threatening letters that Robin left for me?"

"Just another layer to make you miserable. Like I am. But I'm tired of talking about this. Tired of trying to justify myself to you. Call down to your men," Evan ordered. "Tell them to get that car and the cash. And tell them to hurry. My patience is wearing thin."

Jackson didn't move and didn't look back, but he relayed the demand from over his shoulder. He asked them to take the cash that they kept in Steven's office. His men would do as they were told, which meant within minutes Evan would have what he wanted.

And within minutes, Jackson would be ready to take him down when he tried to get out of the house. It was a long way down those stairs. Longer still for Evan to reach the car that would be brought to the driveway. If by some miracle the man did make it to the vehicle, it had a GPS tracking device.

"I had to make you feel how much it hurts to lose someone you love," Evan snarled, his words angry again. "That's why I let you have Caden all this time. I wanted you to love him, and I want your heart ripped to pieces when you lose him."

"Then why take Bailey?" Jackson challenged. He took another step closer. "She had nothing to do with that plane crash. You hurt, and are continuing to hurt, an innocent woman. Let her go."

"No. I can't. She's collateral damage since she gave birth to Caden. I've been following her, you know, and making sure she didn't come to you too soon."

Jackson kept trying. "Too soon?"

"I wanted to drag this out longer. I wanted you to be with Caden a few more months, but then Bailey decided to come here, and that moved up all my plans."

So, Evan had been the one following her, and that's how he knew when to send the first hired gun out to the estate. Since Evan had access to the security cameras both inside and outside the house, that explained how he had been able to pinpoint them so easily during the attacks. It made Jackson sick to think that Evan had been watching all this time.

"Bailey didn't know about your plans," Jackson pressed. "You can make it so she's safe. You too."

"Right." Evan gave another hollow laugh. "The only thing you want is for me to be arrested. Well, that's not going to happen. SAPD would charge me as an accessory to the hostage incident. People were murdered that day, and you and I both know that accessory to murder is the same sentence as murder itself."

Jackson wasn't sure of that at all, but he was certain that Evan would be charged with a whole host of other things that he'd carried out in the past forty-eight hours.

"I have the cash," one of Jackson's men called out from the foyer. "And the car is in front of the house."

"Time to go," Evan said, obviously not wasting any time. "Back up, Jackson. And don't try anything stupid. I have nothing to lose here."

Oh yes he did. Evan was about to lose his life.

But then Jackson saw something that could give this an ugly turn.

Behind Evan and Bailey, there was some movement, and a moment later, he spotted Sheriff Gentry. He was easing up the ladder that Evan had apparently used to gain entry into the nursery. Of course, Evan had been able to do that because he'd shot out the window.

Jackson shook his head slightly so the sheriff would stop. He wanted Gentry's help, but he didn't want Evan getting spooked. Best to get the man onto the stairs where there would be more room to maneuver.

"What?" Evan demanded. It was obvious something alerted him.

Jackson didn't look at the sheriff because he didn't want Evan to follow his gaze. But he must have sensed that someone was behind him.

A sound tore from Evan's mouth. Not exactly a shout. Something that sounded more animal than human.

Evan turned, dragging Bailey with him. Both of them moving to face the sheriff.

Hell.

Evan's hand tightened, poised to pull the trigger of the gun still pointed at Bailey's head.

Jackson still didn't have a clean shot, so he lowered his head and dove toward Bailey and Evan. It was a huge risk. The biggest one he'd ever taken, but he couldn't just stand there while Evan fired.

He plowed right into them and sent all three of them crashing against what was left of the window frame. Bits of wood and glass flew everywhere. So did Evan's hands. The man was trying to bash the gun and his fist into anything close enough for him to hurt.

Jackson couldn't stop Evan's fist from bashing into Bailey's stomach.

And then there was the shot.

The sound of it blasted through the room.

Bailey gasped, as if fighting for air, and Jackson saw her crumple to the floor. God, had she been hit? Had he lost her?

And in that moment of fear and panic, he realized just what she meant to him.

"Bailey!" Jackson shouted, but his voice was drowned out by the other sounds.

The echo from the gunshot. The chaos that followed.

The rustling of the sheriff diving through the window to grab hold of Evan. But Jackson didn't hear the one sound he wanted to hear.

He didn't hear Bailey's voice.

Chapter Eighteen

Bailey heard everything, every sound of the struggle going on around her. She could see, too. But what she couldn't do was speak. That's because the breath had been knocked out of her when Evan punched her in the stomach.

Jackson cursed, something raw and filled with fury. He came at Evan and latched onto the man's hand so he couldn't fire his gun again. Jackson bashed Evan's hand against the floor, and when he didn't let go of the weapon, he bashed it again.

Finally, Evan dropped the gun.

The sheriff was right there to grab the man and pin him down so that he couldn't move and go after that gun again.

Bailey tried to get up, but Jackson beat her to it. He raced to her and scooped her up into his arms.

"Are you hurt?" he demanded.

She managed to shake her head, but her voice still wouldn't cooperate.

That's because she saw the blood.

It was trickling down the side of Jackson's face.

"But *you're* hurt," she said.

It seemed to take much too long for her to reach up

and wipe away the blood. Not a gunshot wound, thank God. It had likely come from the broken glass.

The relief was overwhelming. Maybe because it was mixed with the adrenaline and the realization that they had both come out of this alive.

Bailey grabbed Jackson and kissed him.

She didn't bother to keep it simple and sweet. It was a kiss filled with the powerful emotions coursing through her.

"She's okay, I guess," the sheriff mumbled, sounding mildly amused. He hauled Evan to his feet. "I got an update from SAPD on the way over. They have the woman they're calling hostage number four, and everything seems resolved. She's safe, and there isn't going to be another hostage incident. Turned out to be a ruse."

Thank God. It was all over, except for dealing with the aftermath of the situation that Evan and his hired guns had created.

"Your men got the third intruder," the sheriff continued, "and he's spilling his guts, already trying to work out a deal so he can testify against Mr. Young here in exchange for immunity."

"That little weasel," Evan snarled. "I knew I couldn't trust him."

"He said you didn't pay him nearly enough." The sheriff handcuffed Evan. "He also said you were the mastermind of this disaster, that you'd hired not just him but the other gunman, and that you came here to kill Bailey and then kidnap the child."

Evan cursed, but he didn't deny any of it. Good reason. There was a ton of evidence against him.

"And the explosions?" Jackson asked. Bailey was

thankful he'd asked. She wanted to know about those as well.

"I wanted to distract you so I could get inside," Evan spat out. "I should have blown up the house and everyone in it instead."

The man's venom caused Bailey to shudder.

"We have Shannon Wright and Robin Russo down at my office," Sheriff Gentry added. "I put them in protective custody just about the same time I got a call about this attack here at the estate. I don't think either woman had any part in this."

Well, that was something, at least. Still, it would no doubt take a while for Shannon to get her life back in order. And of course, Robin would face charges for taking Caden and for leaving those threatening letters.

"What about Ryan Cassaine?" Bailey asked.

The sheriff shook his head. "No links to this one here," he said, tipping his head to Evan. Sheriff Gentry mumbled something about that being a good thing, and he led Evan out the door.

Bailey looked away from the man who'd made her life a living hell. She didn't want another glimpse of him. She only wanted Evan and his dead henchman out of the house.

"I'm so sorry," Jackson whispered.

"For what? This wasn't your fault."

"Evan worked for me," Jackson pointed out.

"And you had no idea that his fiancée's death made him crazy. No. I won't let you take the blame for this."

"Thank you for that." Jackson gathered her in his

arms and kissed her right back. That robbed her of what little breath she'd managed to gather.

He pulled back. Met her gaze. "Let's check on Caden." Jackson took her hand and hurried out the door and toward the back stairs.

Bailey suddenly couldn't get to Caden fast enough. The only consolation in all of this was that her baby was too young to remember the attack that had almost cost him his parents.

"We're his parents," she mumbled.

Jackson's grip tightened on her hand. "What did you say?"

"We're Caden's parents," she said a little louder.

She hadn't expected him to come to a dead stop outside the panic room and whirl around to face her again. He suddenly looked like a dark warrior ready for another battle. The muscles in his jaw stirred, and he stared at her with narrowed, waiting eyes.

"Yes. We are." His voice was as clogged with emotion as hers. Jackson didn't seem the ruthless businessman now. He seemed humbled. "You aren't going to take him from me, are you?"

It was such a heartfelt question that it brought tears to her eyes. "No." But until she heard her answer, she hadn't been sure what was going to happen next.

She still wasn't.

It was almost as if she were still out of breath, waiting. Because Bailey figured what she said and did here in the next few minutes would change her life forever.

A scary thought.

Her head was filled with all the images of the attack, and there was still some blood on Jackson's forehead.

She could hear Evan's threats. The explosions. The shots that had been fired.

But for some reason, her mind was crystal-clear.

"We can share custody," she suggested, though that didn't sound as good as it should have. "It's a reasonable solution."

"Reasonable," Jackson repeated. He shook his head, cursed. "What if I don't want reasonable?"

Bailey blinked, and there went the air again. "You can't want full custody?"

He shook his head again. Cursed again. He reached for the button that would open the monitor for the panic room but then jerked back his hand.

"I do want full custody," he insisted. "And I also want you."

Because she was gearing up for a fight, and trying to figure out how she was going to deal with a broken heart, it took a moment for that to sink in.

"You want me?" she clarified, not sure exactly what he meant by that.

He put his hands on his hips. "Not an affair. Not just sex. *You.*"

Which still didn't clarify everything.

She must have looked confused, because he grasped her shoulders and stared at her. And it seemed as if he just couldn't find the right words. Strange. Jackson had a knack for saying and doing the right thing at the right time.

"I'm in love with you," Bailey blurted out. Yes, it was a massive risk. It could be too much too soon for the Texas tycoon, but Bailey didn't regret it. He needed the facts, and the facts were that she was desperately in love with him.

He didn't respond. Instead, he let go of her and pushed the button so the monitor would drop down.

"How's Caden?" Jackson asked, the moment that Tracy's image appeared on the screen.

"Sleeping." Tracy stepped back so they could see him.

Caden was indeed asleep, snuggled into his blanket as if this was an ordinary night. It wasn't. They'd just been attacked, and she'd just poured out her heart to Jackson and had gotten no response.

"Is it safe to come out?" Tracy asked.

Jackson nodded, and a moment later the thick steel door opened. "Could you let everyone know that the crisis is over, that they can return to their quarters?"

"Certainly." Tracy didn't linger. She hurried away, obviously relieved that the danger was gone.

She and Jackson stepped inside and tiptoed across the room. Bailey went to the crib and stared down at her son. She got that same warm jolt every time she looked at Caden, and it was even stronger now.

"I wanted to say this here, with Caden in the room," Jackson whispered. He slid his hand over hers.

Since he didn't seem eager to continue, Bailey just decided to put her fear right out there so she could try to deal with it. "You're dumping me?"

Jackson looked as if she'd slapped him. "No." He didn't have any trouble getting that out. Nor moving. He pulled her closer to him and turned her so they were face-to-face.

"Dumping you?" he asked, making it sound like the last thing on his mind. "I was going to tell you that I'm in love with you, too. And then I was going to ask you to marry me."

Now it was Bailey's turn to be stunned. *Mercy.* She hadn't seen that coming.

"You really were going to do those things?" she asked.

Jackson winced. "I still am." He stared at her. "I love you. And—will you marry me?"

Bailey wanted to say yes. Heck, she wanted to jump for joy, kiss Jackson and then haul him off to bed somewhere. But she couldn't just go blindly into this.

"No," Jackson interrupted before she could say anything. "I'm not doing this for Caden. Or even for us. I'm doing it for me. I want you, not just for tonight. And not just to be Caden's mother. Bailey, I want *you* because I love *you.*"

She studied his eyes, looking for any signs of doubt, but there weren't any.

Bailey only saw the love, and it was the same love that she felt in her heart.

She smiled, slid her hand around the back of Jackson's neck and pulled him down for a kiss. It wasn't the frantic kiss of relief she'd given him in the aftermath of the attack. This one was meant to say only one thing.

I love you.

Still, Bailey gave him the words to go along with the kiss. "I love you, Jackson. And yes, I'll marry you."

He smiled, but she caught that smile with her mouth and tasted it with another kiss.

Like their other kissing sessions, this one turned hot very fast, and Jackson hauled her against him so they were body-to-body and touching everywhere. It left her breathless and wanting a whole lot more.

"I have no doubts that this is how I want to spend the rest of my life," she whispered. "With you and Caden."

At the sound of his name, Caden started to fuss. But

not just fuss. He woke up and started to wail. It was loud and a complete attention-getter.

At the same time, they reached for him—and then laughed when they bumped into each other. Caden stopped crying and stared at them as if trying to figure out why they were so darn happy when he was cranky over having his sleep interrupted with a marriage proposal and a declaration of love ever after.

Bailey stepped back a little so that Jackson could pick up the baby. He kissed Caden's cheek and then handed the baby to her.

"She said yes," Jackson whispered in Caden's ear. "Your mom is going to be my wife. And if we play our cards right, one day you might get a little sister or brother out of this deal."

Even though Caden couldn't have possibly understood what he meant, he must have picked up on his dada's happy tone and expression.

Caden smiled, a big gummy grin complete with a "Coo."

Their son obviously approved, and to celebrate, Bailey gave both of them another kiss.

This was her dream come true. The life she had always wanted. And it was right in her arms, and in her heart, forever.

* * * * *

Don't miss
THE TEXAS LAWMAN'S LAST STAND,
the final book in Delores Fossen's miniseries,
TEXAS MATERNITY: LABOR AND DELIVERY.
Look for it wherever
Harlequin Intrigue books are sold.

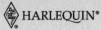 HARLEQUIN®

INTRIGUE

COMING NEXT MONTH

Available January 11, 2011

REQUEST YOUR FREE BOOKS!

2 FREE NOVELS
PLUS 2
FREE GIFTS!

✦ HARLEQUIN®

INTRIGUE®

Breathtaking Romantic Suspense

YES! Please send me 2 FREE Harlequin Intrigue® novels and my 2 FREE gifts (gifts are worth about $10). After receiving them, if I don't wish to receive any more books, I can return the shipping statement marked "cancel." If I don't cancel, I will receive 6 brand-new novels every month and be billed just $4.24 per book in the U.S. or $4.99 per book in Canada. That's a saving of at least 15% off the cover price! It's quite a bargain! Shipping and handling is just 50¢ per book.* I understand that accepting the 2 free books and gifts places me under no obligation to buy anything. I can always return a shipment and cancel at any time. Even if I never buy another book from Harlequin, the two free books and gifts are mine to keep forever.

182/382 HDN E5MG

Name _____
            (PLEASE PRINT)

Address _____ Apt. # _____

City _____ State/Prov. _____ Zip/Postal Code _____

Signature (if under 18, a parent or guardian must sign) _____

Mail to the **Harlequin Reader Service:**
IN U.S.A.: P.O. Box 1867, Buffalo, NY 14240-1867
IN CANADA: P.O. Box 609, Fort Erie, Ontario L2A 5X3
Not valid for current subscribers to Harlequin Intrigue books.

**Are you a subscriber to Harlequin Intrigue books and
want to receive the larger-print edition? Call 1-800-873-8635 today!**

* Terms and prices subject to change without notice. Prices do not include applicable taxes. N.Y. residents add applicable sales tax. Canadian residents will be charged applicable provincial taxes and GST. Offer not valid in Quebec. This offer is limited to one order per household. All orders subject to approval. Credit or debit balances in a customer's account(s) may be offset by any other outstanding balance owed by or to the customer. Please allow 4 to 6 weeks for delivery. Offer available while quantities last.

Your Privacy: Harlequin is committed to protecting your privacy. Our Privacy Policy is available online at www.eHarlequin.com or upon request from the Reader Service. From time to time we make our lists of customers available to reputable third parties who may have a product or service of interest to you. If you would prefer we not share your name and address, please check here. ☐

Help us get it right—We strive for accurate, respectful and relevant communications. To clarify or modify your communication preferences, visit us at www.ReaderService.com/consumerschoice.

H110R

HARLEQUIN®

A Romance

FOR EVERY MOOD™

Spotlight on

Classic

Quintessential, modern love stories
that are romance at its finest.

See the next page
to enjoy a sneak peek from
the Harlequin Presents® series.

Harlequin Presents® *is thrilled*
to introduce the first installment of
an epic tale of passion and drama by
USA TODAY Bestselling Author
Penny Jordan!

When buttoned-up Giselle first meets
the devastatingly handsome Saul Parenti,
the heat between them is explosive....

"LET ME GET THIS STRAIGHT. Are you actually suggesting that I would stoop to that kind of game playing?"

Saul came out from behind his desk and walked toward her. Giselle could smell his hot male scent and it was making her dizzy, igniting a low, dull, pulsing ache that was taking over her whole body.

Giselle defended her suspicions. "You don't want me here."

"No," Saul agreed, "I don't."

And then he did what he had sworn he would not do, cursing himself beneath his breath as he reached for her, pulling her fiercely into his arms and kissing her with all the pent-up fury she had aroused in him from the moment he had first seen her.

Giselle certainly *wanted* to resist him. But the hand she raised to push him away developed a will of its own and was sliding along his bare arm beneath the sleeve of his shirt, and the body that should have been arching away from him was instead melting into him.

Beneath the pressure of his kiss he could feel and taste her gasp of undeniable response to him. He wanted to devour her, take her and drive them both until they were equally satiated—even whilst the anger within him that she should make him feel that way roared and burned its resentment of his need.

She was helpless, Giselle recognized, totally unable to withstand the storm lashing at her, able only to cling to the man who was the cause of it and pray that she would survive.

Somewhere else in the building a door banged. The sound exploded into the sensual tension that had enclosed them, driving them apart. Saul's chest was rising and falling as he fought for control; Giselle's whole body was trembling.

Without a word she turned and ran.

Find out what happens when Saul and Giselle succumb to their irresistible desire in

THE RELUCTANT SURRENDER

Available January 2011 from Harlequin Presents®

ROMANTIC
SUSPENSE

Sparked by Danger, Fueled by Passion.

NEW YORK TIMES BESTSELLING AUTHOR

RACHEL LEE

No Ordinary Hero

Strange noises...a woman's mysterious disappearance
and a killer on the loose who's too close for comfort.

With no where else to turn, Delia Carmody looks
to her aloof neighbour to help, only to discover
that Mike Windwalker is no ordinary hero.

Conard County THE NEXT GENERATION

Available in December.
Wherever books are sold.

Visit Silhouette Books at www.eHarlequin.com

SRS27709R